THE SONG OF PERCIVAL PEACOCK

A NOVEL BY RUSSELL EDSON

# The Song of
# Percival Peacock

COFFEE HOUSE PRESS :: MINNEAPOLIS :: 1992

The author wishes to thank The Mrs. Giles Whiting Foundation for its support and encouragement during the preparation of this book.

The publisher extends thanks to Bush Foundation; Dayton Hudson Foundation; Minnesota State Arts Board; the National Endowment for the Arts, a federal agency; and Northwest Area Foundation for support of this project.

Coffee House Press books are available to bookstores through our primary distributor, Consortium Book Sales & Distribution, 287 East Sixth St., Suite 365, St. Paul, Minnesota 55101. Our books are also available through all major library distributors and jobbers, and through most small press distributors, including Bookpeople, Book-slinger, Inland, and Small Press Distribution. For personal orders, catalogs or other information, write to:
Coffee House Press
27 North Fourth Street, Suite 400, Minneapolis, MN 55401

Library of Congress Cataloging-in-Publication Data

Edson, Russell.
        The song of Percival Peacock : a novel / by Russell Edson.
            p. cm.
        ISBN 1-56689-002-0 (pbk.) : $11.95
            I. Title.
PS3509.D58S66 1992
813'.54 — dc20
                    92-22804
                    CIP

*for Frances*

# Peacock Arrives

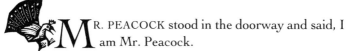MR. PEACOCK stood in the doorway and said, I am Mr. Peacock.

The Caretaker yawned and said, I thought you were dead.

I am the young Peacock, cried Mr. Peacock.

Another one? said the Caretaker.

As much as any branch reaching from a tree with hungry twigs, said Mr. Peacock.

The Caretaker yawned.

Where is my throne? cried Mr. Peacock.

Throne? sighed the Caretaker.

The estate inventory lists 137 chairs, but there's a question mark next to the 37th, cried Mr. Peacock.

It's just a chair, whimpered the Caretaker.

It is not just a chair, it's symbolic; it creates the rent out of which all things flow away, yelled Mr. Peacock.

Please don't yell at me, said the Caretaker.

I'm not yelling, yelled Mr. Peacock.

You are yelling, cried the Caretaker.

But I'm upset. I always yell when I'm upset. Surely you understand that under these conditions I am justified in yelling, yelled Mr. Peacock.

But I feel bad when you yell; like you were yelling at me, sighed the Caretaker.

Well, weren't you supposed to watch over the house? yelled Mr. Peacock.

We thought the last Peafowl had died. We had no idea another Peacock would appear. Oh, do stop yelling! yelled the Caretaker.

Now you're yelling, screamed Mr. Peacock.

I can't help it, you're making me nervous with your yelling, yelled the Caretaker.

Shut up, how dare you yell at me? yelled Mr. Peacock.

I'm not yelling at you, I'm yelling because I'm nervous, yelled the Caretaker.

You have no right to be nervous, you have lost nothing, screamed Mr. Peacock.

It is true, I have lost nothing; but I have become nervous because of your yelling, yelled the Caretaker.

Servants must have control. They must not let themselves go to pieces. Those in authority, with responsibility need the moral support of quiet and efficient servants, screamed Mr. Peacock.

I thought the last Peafowl was dead, wept the Caretaker.

Well, you can plainly see the last Peacock is still erect, screamed Mr. Peacock.


Easy, easy, gentlemen, said a voice from the stairway.

Who is this person? cried Mr. Peacock.

That's the Maid, cried the Caretaker.

The Maid? cried Mr. Peacock.

Tell him who you are, said the Caretaker.

I'm the Maid, said the Maid.

This is Mr. Peacock, said the Caretaker.

So? . . . said the Maid.

So this is my house, cried Mr. Peacock.

Well, what of that? said the Maid.

I want respect, screamed Mr. Peacock.

Now don't get excited, dearie, said the Maid.

I am very excited, screamed Mr. Peacock.

Mr. Kneesock is very excited, said the Caretaker.

So?. . . said the Maid.

So I am very excited, screamed Mr. Peacock.

Well, I only work here, you'll have to see the master, said the Maid.

I am the master, screamed Mr. Peacock.

Well, all right, if you want to be the boss, that's all right, sighed the Maid.

I want action, screamed Mr. Peacock.

Well, whatcha want me to do? I can't move too fast. Just look at me and you'll understand . . . These feet. I have lots of trouble with these feet. I suppose it's overweight does it. But what am I to do? sighed the Maid.

Mr. Peacock is the last of the Peafowls, said the Caretaker.

I see . . . , said the Maid.

You see what? screamed Mr. Peacock.

Just a figure of speech, said the Maid.

Where is the missing chair? said Mr. Peacock.

Oh, that's a whole story in itself, said the Maid.

Just tell me what happened, yelled Mr. Peacock.

It's hard to tell where it all began, sighed the Maid.

Well, begin someplace, roared Mr. Peacock.

It's because you Peafowls died out. Yes, I blame the whole thing on death, said the Maid.

Death? screamed Mr. Peacock.

The child of death, grief . . . Well, as you probably know, the last of the Peafowls died . . . , sighed the Maid.

Not quite, Miss old-fat-woman, there is still one abroad.

That is yet to be proved, said the Maid.

Get on with it, screamed Mr. Peacock.


## ABOUT OLD MR. PEACOCK

Old Mr. Sickcock took to bed. We said, sir, that's not nice. He had become rather childish. And though he was many years older than I, still, in some way he filled a certain maternal need in me. Wouldn't you like to get up and play, dear? I said to him. He looked awfully limp and wrinkled. Come, dear, give me your hand, I coaxed. I asked the Caretaker if we shouldn't call a doctor. He said, why? And, not being able to think of an answer, I let the matter rest, said the Maid.

You mean you didn't call a doctor? screamed Mr. Peacock.

Well, sometimes I would go to the window and call out. But no one heard me, said the Maid.

Why didn't you go to town and fetch a doctor? screamed Mr. Peacock.

Look at these feet. I have an awful lot of trouble with these feet, said the Maid.

What about the Caretaker, why didn't he go? screamed Mr. Peacock.

It was my day off; I said to old Mr. Palecock, if you can just hold on until tomorrow . . . , said the Caretaker.

Tomorrow?! Why must everything be put off until tomorrow? That's the trouble with servants, it's always tomorrow, screamed Mr. Peacock.

Well, sir, we didn't, of course, have the personal interest that a member of the family might. Although I've seen some families where you would have thought they were all strangers, said the Caretaker.

What has that to do with it? screamed Mr. Peacock.

I was just saying . . . , said the Caretaker.

Finish up about the chair. All this talk about old Mr. Peacock is neither here nor there. I never knew him, so what interest is it to me all these details? said Mr. Peacock.

Just to add a little background surrounding the chair's disappearance, said the Maid.

Okay okay, go on, screamed Mr. Peacock.


## MAYONNAISE

Well, you understand that I have rheumatism, sighed the Maid.

So what! screamed Mr. Peacock.

Please, sir, you mustn't shout, said the Maid.

It's my house, I can shout if I wish, screamed Mr. Peacock.

I was trying to say that because of my rheumatism I like to undress in the kitchen, and put mayonnaise on my body, and just let it soak in. It's necessary for me to completely undress, said the Maid.

Yes yes, you're covered with mayonnaise and naked, screamed Mr. Peacock.

You're talking so loudly I can barely gather my thoughts, said the Maid.

I'm all nerves, screamed Mr. Peacock.

I've told the Caretaker to keep out of the kitchen a thousand times. So many times I caught old Mr. Hardcock by the window peeking in, said the Maid.

I don't want to appear rude. And I sympathize with your maidenly modesty. It's perfectly natural your not wanting to be viewed with mayonnaise all over you. But I'm very anxious about the missing chair, said Mr. Peacock.

Yes, I'm coming to that. As you might remember I was saying that old Mr. Sickcock was upstairs dying. Yet, I see no reason, even in times of death, not to medicate the living. So I was in the kitchen covering myself with mayonnaise. And the Caretaker kept coming into the kitchen with all sorts of excuses for being there. I said, well, all right, but keep your eyes closed. I said, get what you want and get out. Then I noticed old Mr. Peepingcock, sick as he was, by the window. I thought, sick as he is, he's climbed down the drainpipe to look at me undressed. I said to him, if you don't get back in your bed I'll have the Caretaker give you a spanking, said the Maid.

How does the missing throne figure in all this? yelled Mr. Peacock.

Now that's what I'm getting to. I went out into the yard and made old Mr. Hardcock climb back up the drainpipe. I said, now you get back into bed. As I was coming back to the kitchen door, who do I see but old widow Shoutington. She says, you ought to be ashamed walking around like that, greased up like a physical culturist. I said to her, that ain't nice to make personal remarks; at least I ain't all skinny and mean like you, Mrs. Shoutington. Fat people are usually generous, don't you think so, Mr. Peacock? said the Maid.

I don't know. Fat people just seem to be fat. Will you please stop bringing this conversation down to the personal level. You are, after all, a servant, yelled Mr. Peacock.

Well, Mr. High-&-Mighty, just who do you think you are? said the Maid.

I'm the master! Don't you dare speak to me like that, screamed Mr. Peacock.

I'm a human being too, Mr. Peacock, and old enough to be your mother. And I don't think you have any right to act like Mr. Uppity, said the Maid.

She's right, whimpered the Caretaker.

Right? Right about what? screamed Mr. Peacock.

Well, I'm not sure I understand the charges or allegations . . . Except, that your tone is most unpleasant. You see, sir, the Maid and I have built a rather quiet life here, said the Caretaker.

How dare you build a quiet life in my residence? screamed Mr. Peacock.

The Caretaker means we're not used to being shouted at, said the Maid.

I know what he means. How dare you interpret the Caretaker to me as if I were a child needing special explanations, screamed Mr. Peacock.

Well, you're sure not the man old Mr. Blisscock was. He never raised his voice. Not once did I ever hear him raise his voice, unless he was angry, said the Maid.

Don't you think you're taking a rather personal tone about my relative? yelled Mr. Peacock.

Well, if you don't want us to tell you what happened to the missing chair, I, for one, am not one to volunteer information; that's one thing I ain't is a gossip, bless the Lord, said the Maid.

Tell me what happened to my chair. You tell me everything except what happened to my chair, screamed Mr. Peacock.

Well, I didn't go to no fancy school to learn how to talk good, said the Maid.

I like the way you talk, said the Caretaker.

I don't need you to say that, though I appreciate your saying it, said the Maid.

Shut up, both of you. You will not carry on personal conversations in my presence, screamed Mr. Peacock.

Well, Mr. Bigcock, maybe I just won't tell you what happened to the chair, said the Maid.


## HUMAN NATURE

I might as well warn both of you, now that you've obviously turned against me, you're both a hair's breadth away from being arrested for stealing my chair. Unless you can offer some reasonable explanation as to the disappearance of the chair, you may find your declining years spent behind bars, said Mr. Peacock.

He took it, the Caretaker took it, yelled the Maid.

It was she that took it, whimpered the Caretaker.

I swear on the memory of old Mr. Peacock it was the Caretaker that took the chair, said the Maid.

How dare you swear on the memory of my relative? screamed Mr. Peacock.

That's right, that proves she took it. I loved that chair, I wouldn't do anything to hurt it, whimpered the Caretaker.

How dare you love something belonging to me? screamed Mr. Peacock.

I loved it like a son, whimpered the Caretaker.

I will choke you to death, Mr. Caretaker, or whatever your name is, if I am not properly satisfied as to the whereabouts and safety of my throne, screamed Mr. Peacock.

But I was asleep at the time, whimpered the Caretaker.

How do I know that? screamed Mr. Peacock.

I just told you, said the Caretaker.

But you might be lying, screamed Mr. Peacock.

I never lie, that's something I never do. Steal, maybe, rob once in a while. But lie, that's something I never do, said the Caretaker.

That's right, he never lies, usually. Oh, once in a while; anybody might lie once in a while, said the Maid.

Of course, that's only human . . . Are you trying to explain human nature in the person of the Caretaker? screamed Mr. Peacock.

Oh, no, sir, the Maid did not mean that I was to stand for all humanity, whimpered the Caretaker.

I wish she'd make herself clear. For a moment I felt she was projecting you as a victim of modern industrial society, said Mr. Peacock, whereas, in fact, you are both typical family retainers, both grown slack and greedy for lack of supervision.

We have done our best to maintain the standards set by old Mr. Peahen. Naturally without the impetus of threat, or the catalytic scream, we have let certain things go. For instance, it must be said, in all fairness, that we have let our personal appearances go. What reason have we to look attractive now that old Mr. Alarmclock is dead? said the Maid.

I think you overstate the case when you imply that you are capable of looking more attractive than you do now. I find both you and the Caretaker not only dishevelled, but more, you are fundamentally unattractive. You are grossly overweight and old, and could not in the least arouse any sexual interest, at least from this quarter. The Caretaker is bent, not only by age and unfortunate birth, but spiritually. His humility is actually a whining petulance, said Mr. Peacock.

Which is in no way an argument against regenerative activities, leading perhaps, with a little faith, toward a general improvement to what otherwise appears a general decline in outlook, said the Maid.

I do not wish to go over your faults at this time. This discussion of your persons tends to place us on a level of equality, which at best raises you and lowers me, cried Mr. Peacock.

We're all human, whimpered the Caretaker.

That is the only similarity. After that the divergence becomes too great to even consider further talks toward joining ourselves into a community, screamed Mr. Peacock.

We have no wish to have any closer association, Mr. Kneelock, than exists in the mutual respect of employer and employee, said the Maid.

But I don't respect you at all. How dare you think that I respect you? There is no basis for equal but separate nobilities. I wish to find out about the chair, but instead, I get gossip and ill-considered philosophy from inferiors. May we get on about the throne? screamed Mr. Peacock.

Where was I? said the Maid.

Mrs. Shoutington. You were talking about Mrs. Shoutington, yelled Mr. Peacock.

I can hear perfectly well without your shouting, Mr. Peacock, said the Maid.

Are you correcting me? screamed Mr. Peacock.

I'm trying to say that I can hear you perfectly well without your shouting, said the Maid.

Very well, said Mr. Peacock.

. . . I was saying to Mrs. Shoutington that it wasn't nice to make personal remarks . . . You see, I have rheumatism . . . , said the Maid.

Mrs. Shoutington had insulted you. So what? Do you think I

care in the least if you are insulted? Mrs. Shoutington is obviously your superior. And is, no doubt, quite correct in her estimate of you. I have never heard of a fat old woman walking in the nude, covered with mayonnaise. I let this pass before without judgment because of my breeding. But now that you bring it up a second time I am more than angry at the picture you present. Inviting impure thoughts. Chasing old Mr. Flintlock up his own drain-pipe. What do you take me for, a conspirator in these tasteless adventures you feel called upon to repeat? Surely, these tasteless details have little bearing on the disappearance of my chair. I cannot help wondering if your main purpose is not to stir up wild sexual fantasies in me, leading to my proposing marriage, screamed Mr. Peacock.

Oh, we are brothers. You are suffering as I have suffered in my long courtship of this woman, sighed the Caretaker.

Don't you dare sentimentalize our relationship, screamed Mr. Peacock.

I only meant . . ., whimpered the Caretaker.

Be quiet, I'm trying to listen to the Maid. Now continue, madam, cried Mr. Peacock.

. . . I said, at least I ain't all skinny and mean like you, Mrs. Shoutington. Then I noticed old Mr. Peepeecock looking down at me from the back porch roof. I said to Mrs. Shoutington, don't you think it's insulting the way old Mr. Ticktock looks at me? Mrs. Uppity Shoutington says, do you think I care in the least if you are insulted? Old Mr. Peacock is obviously your superior, and is, no doubt, quite correct in his estimate of you. I said, I'm treating myself for rheumatism. She said, I have never heard of a fat old woman walking about in the nude, covered with mayonnaise. And I might say that I am more than angry at the picture you present; inviting impure thoughts . . . , said the Maid.

What are you saying? You're saying what I said. You are re-peating my correct     words back to me. Are you so stupid that you think I can't remember what I said five minutes ago? This performance of yours begins to point to an underlying guilt, screamed Mr. Peacock.

Well, Mrs. Shoutington said something like that. I just thought I would use the words at hand, said the Maid.

But the words, as you choose to call them, were actually whole phrases and sentences, which do not in any way further or illuminate the story of the missing chair. I wish you would use some editorial discipline over the material presented. You are either vastly more stupid than I had at first realized, or infinitely more clever at covering up your guilt in this affair, screamed Mr. Peacock.

I know I was wrong to go outside without my clothes on. But you see, I ran out to chase old Mr. Windsock up the drainpipe. In his condition he should have been in bed . . . Not to mention my normal maidenly modesty that plays some part here, too, said the Maid.

Small part, I must say; running about the garden completely undressed, said Mr. Peacock.

Well, you see, I have rheumatism, and I use mayonnaise, which I rub all over. . . , said the Maid.

Shut up. I don't want to hear the sordid reasons for your abuse of good taste, screamed Mr. Peacock.

Oh, I suppose you've never had a sick day in your life. Small wonder with your money. People like me get rheumatism from waiting on people like you, said the Maid.

Shut up this minute, or I'll choke you to death, screamed Mr. Peacock.

Easy, sir, I see a look in you I don't like. The look of a man who's been a long time unhappy. And it's made him mean, said the Maid.

I'm sorry for going all to pieces this way, said Mr. Peacock.

There there, everything's going to be all right, said the Maid.

It's the chair, it's got me very upset, said Mr. Peacock.

We'll get it back. The Caretaker'll get his gun and shoot it down. We'll get it back. It's someplace out there, said the Maid.

Don't worry, sir, I'll kill it and bring it home, said the Caretaker.

I don't want you to ruin my property with your gun, cried Mr. Peacock.

No no, dear, he'll just frighten it and make it come home, said the Maid.

# THE CHILD

Something awful has happened, hasn't it? said Mr. Peacock.

Now don't you trouble your pretty little head about it, said the Maid.

Pretty little head? What kind of talk is that? That's what you say to a little girl, cried Mr. Peacock.

Now now, Mr. Shecock, mama knows best, said the Maid.

I don't think I like your personal tone. I am, after all, a grown man. It's insulting to be spoken to like a child. Particularly by a serving woman, said Mr. Peacock.

She didn't mean anything by that, said the Caretaker.

Be quiet, cried Mr. Peacock.

Why, the first time I saw you I thought to myself, if I had a son he'd be just like you, said the Caretaker.

Like me? Do you think your stringy ignorant loins could bring forth a person of my quality? You are both forgetting your positions, screamed Mr. Peacock.

Now now, sleepy-head, you're getting all excited, said the Maid.

Why do you call me sleepy-head? Do you think you are talking to a child, screamed Mr. Peacock.

You're getting all cranky because you're tired, said the Maid.

I'm not tired. I'm as fully awake as you and father. Now see what you made me say! You made me call the Caretaker, father, screamed Mr. Peacock.

If you were my daughter I'd beat you with a strap until you begged for mercy, cried the Maid.

Why? What did I do? cried Mr. Peacock.

You've been asking for disciplinary action all day; the way you've been talking to your parents, said the Maid.

You are not my parents. You are a serving woman and a serving man. And I am the master here. How dare you suggest that I need a spanking? You're not dealing with old Mr. Peacock, who was easily spanked. No siree! You forget my heft. I could as easily choke the two of you to death as kill a fly, screamed Mr. Peacock.

Mr. Wetfrock, I don't want any violence with you. I should like you to feel welcome here. The Caretaker and I have built quiet lives. We are not used to loud voices and threats of violence. However, we're fully capable of giving a good account of ourselves in a fight. But we hope it will not come to that, said the Maid.

Come to that? Why, I'll throw the both of you out this very night if you get funny with me, cried Mr. Peacock.

Now there's no reason to get all excited. You're getting yourself all worked up. And for what? Please let me tell you about Mrs. Shoutington . . . , said the Maid.

But I've been waiting to hear about my chair, said Mr. Peacock.

But that's what I've been trying to tell you, said the Maid.

All right, all right, go on, cried Mr. Peacock.

Well, as you remember, when we left the story, old Mr. Sickcock was on the porch roof looking down at me. And, if you remember, I hadn't any clothes on, due to the medication being applied to my infirmity. I shouted up to old Mr. Pistoutcock, you're dying, and if you die out there we'll have to call the fire department to get you down. Meanwhile, Mrs. Shoutington was insulting my figure. It's a lot better than yours, Miss Skinny Stringbean, I said. I said to old Mr. Peafowl, now climb back through the window and get into your bed. It's nice to die in bed. He just kept looking at me. And by then the Caretaker began looking around the corner of the house. I said to the Caretaker, go on up and get the Peahen into his room. I yelled up to old Mr. Naughtycock, the Caretaker's going to give you a spanking if you don't behave. Meanwhile, Mrs. Shoutington had slipped into the house. Now I wonder what she wants? I thought. And what do you think? said the Maid.

How do I know? And by the way, can't you cut some of the detail out? cried Mr. Peacock.

I know what she wanted, cried the Caretaker.

I didn't ask you, smartypants, said the Maid.

Well, what did she want? screamed Mr. Peacock.

Well, there she was in the kitchen without a blessed thing on, all covered with mayonnaise. I said to her, what kind of a house do you think I'm running? Now you get your things on and get out of here as fast as you can. I told her she was just going to make the Caretaker wild. He gets all excited by naked women; don't you? said the Maid.

That's not true, whimpered the Caretaker.

I don't give a damn what his reactions are to naked women, screamed Mr. Peacock.

Well, he gets funny. And I had my hands full with old Mr. Ticktock. So I said to Mrs. Shoutington, this ain't no hospital. You go home and use your own mayonnaise. Old Mr. Peafowl is under no obligation to keep you in mayonnaise. She said, I have a better figure than you. This, as she shook her shrivelly, mean hips at me. I said, you ain't got no flesh, no woman flesh. She said at least she didn't look like a Japanese wrestler. Meanwhile, the Caretaker had come into the kitchen. And she asked him which of us got the best figure. And what did you say, you mean mouth? said the Maid.

I was merely trying to be polite in an otherwise completely embarrassing situation, sighed the Caretaker.

You got no loyalty, that's all I can say. Old Mr. Ficklecock and us were like family, said the Maid.

Please spare me these sordid sentimental reflections on the elder Peacock's household. I do not deny that when the master grows weak servants will tend to take over. Among cowards the only act of strength is the preying on those even weaker and more cowardly . . . , said Mr. Peacock.

You don't really understand, sir, in spite of your fine education and other cultural achievements, said the Maid.

This personal tone you use, as if you were addressing a child, is most distressing. I wish you would remember your place. I am becoming extremely tired of having to remind you, said Mr. Peacock.

But, sir, you don't fully grasp what it was like with old Mr. Horsecock. Why, the Caretaker and I were like his parents. Though he was much our senior, still, in his senility he was like a child; an *old* child. And we loved him like a child. We spanked him not out of revenge, but for his own good. I used to comb the white fringe of his hair with every bit of the tenderness any mother would have combed her child's hair. I kissed and tucked him in every night, said the Maid.

However, these sordid details, be they true or not, tend to cast an undignified light on me. For there is an implication in your tone that I too can be handled like a child. But I assure you, I am fully capable of handling my own affairs. And that I will handle my own affairs. And that I will allow no intimacy to develop between us, said Mr. Peacock.

We have no wish to take on another ward. We are well rid of our burden, and quite content to continue our quiet lives; sipping brandy before the fire in the evening, said the Maid.

You shall not sip brandy. And you shall not sit before the fire. You shall be in the servants' quarters on call should I ring for service, cried Mr. Peacock.

We'll see about that, said the Maid.

Oh, no we won't, this is my house. In future I shall make all decisions, screamed Mr. Peacock.

No one can predict the future, sir. One cannot say what will happen, said the Maid.

I'm not talking about prophecy. I'm talking about what I shall demand. Do you think for a moment that I would sit around with servants, sipping fine brandy? cried Mr. Peacock.

Sometimes servants become more than servants, and masters become less than masters. Loneliness builds many bridges, said the maid.

I am not lonely; nor was I trained in bridge building, screamed Mr. Peacock.

The future must happen as it happens, said the Maid.

I'm going to call the police and let them find out what happened to my chair. I thought we could work together without calling in the police. But I see now that I am faced with two conspirators, cried Mr. Peacock.

You must do what you think best, said the Maid.

You're not going to call the police, are you Mr. Padlock? cried the Caretaker.

You will consider yourselves under arrest, and confine yourselves to your quarters, said Mr. Peacock.

# Peacock Calls the Police

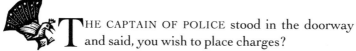THE CAPTAIN OF POLICE stood in the doorway and said, you wish to place charges?

Yes, I most certainly do, screamed Mr. Peacock.

You seem unusually agitated. I do wish you would lower your voice, said the Captain.

I'm very upset, screamed Mr. Peacock.

I know, but there's no reason to scream. You're solving nothing by screaming, said the Captain.

You don't think I want to scream? screamed Mr. Peacock.

Mr. Peacock, I must ask you to lower your voice, said the Captain.

Excuse me, I'm sorry for screaming, screamed Mr. Peacock.

It's all right, now calm down, said the Captain.

Yes, you're right, but I get carried away by injustice, screamed Mr. Peacock.

You're still screaming, yelled the Captain.

You're yelling yourself, screamed Mr. Peacock.

Because you're beginning to make me nervous, screamed the Captain.

A policeman is supposed to be calm even if a civilian goes to pieces, cried Mr. Peacock.

You are not making a friend of me, yelled the Captain.

Are you threatening me? screamed Mr. Peacock.

I am merely saying that no one knows who the guilty party will turn out to be, cried the Captain.

I can assure you, sir, that I can account for every minute of my life, said Mr. Peacock.

Be that as it may, tell me your side of the story, said the Captain.

My side? You seem to imply that there are two sides, cried Mr. Peacock.

You don't think I'm going to shoot the Maid and the Caretaker on your say-so, do you? After all, the Maid has been like a mother to me. Not to mention the Caretaker, who has been like a father to me, cried the Captain.

Oh, well, if it's a family thing I haven't got a chance, screamed Mr. Peacock.

Oh, no, I could easily see you as a sister, or even an aunt. I make these adjustments very easily. I assure you, I love justice more than anything, cried the Captain.

Well, then execute the Maid and the Caretaker, cried Mr. Peacock.

Will you please state the charges you're bringing against them, said the Captain.

I accuse them of willfully and maliciously stealing a kitchen chair, said Mr. Peacock.

A kitchen chair? said the Captain.

Well, I understand that sometimes it appeared in the old Peacock's bedroom. And in that case it was called a bedroom chair. It probably appeared in a variety of rooms, changing its title with each change of address. However, it did at all times belong to this household, said Mr. Peacock.

May I have a list of persons associated with this household? said the Captain.

There was the old Peacock, who having died was replaced by me, another Peacock. Then, of course, these two, said Mr. Peacock.

So there are three Homo sapiens housed under this roof? said the Captain.

Yes yes yes! What are all these questions for? It should be stated that two thieves and one whose chair has been stolen, abide under this roof, screamed Mr. Peacock.

You're screaming again, said the Captain.

Because you're making me nervous with these tedious questions, screamed Mr. Peacock.

I do wish you would stop that screaming. People who raise their voices are usually guilty, said the Captain.

I beg you to remember that you are only a creature of bureaucracy, and therefore, to desist from these personal remarks you seem so fond of making, screamed Mr. Peacock.

I'm terribly sorry that you should look upon my corrective remarks as personal insults. They are given only as a father might advise his daughter, said the Captain.

How dare you attempt to advise me? I asked you here only as a servant whose specialty is brutality, to handle the ugly job of punishing wicked servants, screamed Mr. Peacock.

I am a servant of the people, not your personal servant. Which means I am also the servant of your servants, until they are proven guilty, said the Captain.

I want you to hit them with your nightstick. That's your job, screamed Mr. Peacock.

I'm afraid, sir, unless you lower your voice I shall be forced to leave. I am not a psychiatrist, said the Captain.

Oh, so now it comes out, you're a doctor disguised as a policeman, screamed Mr. Peacock.

Before I go deaf, if you're placing charges against the Maid and the Caretaker, do so, and I'll take them away for trial, said the Captain.

Thank you, said Mr. Peacock.

But what are the charges, Mr. Peacock? said the Captain.

Chair stealing, screamed Mr. Peacock.

# Peacock Visited by
# Mrs. Shoutington

MRS. SHOUTINGTON stood in the doorway. . .
Come in, Mrs. Shoutington, so glad to meet
you, cried Mr. Peacock.

Thank you for asking me over, Mr. Peacock, said Mrs. Shoutington.

I've had a great deal of trouble with the servants since I came
here, said Mr. Peacock.

You mean the Maid. She's a terrible person, with an even worse
figure, said Mrs. Shoutington.

I have reason to believe that she and the Caretaker stole one of
my chairs, said Mr. Peacock.

Oh, the Caretaker, he's a most unattractive person, cried Mrs. Shoutington.

I don't trust him at all, said Mr. Peacock.

The Maid has always envied my figure, said Mrs. Shoutington.

I had them arrested, said Mr. Peacock.

Oh, good for you, cried Mrs. Shoutington.

There was nothing else I could do after I became convinced that they stole the chair, said Mr. Peacock.

I suppose you've noticed how she's let herself go? said Mrs. Shoutington.

You mean how she's lost all respect for persons in superior positions? said Mr. Peacock.

No no, I mean her figure. She's let herself go to fat. I don't think any man would find her very attractive, do you, Mr. Fatcock? said Mrs. Shoutington.

Mrs. Shoutington, I'm not used to looking at servants in that way, cried Mr. Peacock.

Oh, really? I thought all men looked at all women that way, said Mrs. Shoutington.

Mrs. Shoutington, I consider servants as nonentities, cried Mr. Peacock.

The way she's let her figure go I don't blame you, Mr. Hecock, said Mrs. Shoutington.

I've asked you here to help me. You see, I can't seem to get any information out of the servants. They're obviously covering up their crime. But I understand you were a good friend of the elder Peacock and spent a good deal of time here. Perhaps you know something that might help me? said Mr. Peacock.

I'll say one thing, old Mr. Pisscock liked me better than the Maid. You have only to look at her to see why. Why, she's let herself go completely to fat. He admired the way I kept myself. It only takes a little self-respect, said Mrs. Shoutington.

Mrs. Shoutington, I must ask you to stop dwelling on the physical aspects of the Maid. I do not consider her a woman in the sense that I would consider a female of my own class. To me she is merely a female entity, in the sense of a female dog, a bitch, as it were, cried Mr. Peacock.

A bitch! Exactly, Mr. Petcock. That describes her exactly. The nerve of that bitch . . . , shouted Mrs. Shoutington.

What are you saying? Your language . . .,.screamed Mr. Peacock.

You called her a bitch yourself, cried Mrs. Shoutington.

I did not. I did not, screamed Mr. Peacock.

Why are you screaming at me? screamed Mrs. Shoutington.

Because you keep talking about the Maid on a personal level. I don't care for her as a woman. She is merely a serving person who commits crimes, screamed Mr. Peacock.

Well, you needn't scream, screamed Mrs. Shoutington.

You're screaming yourself, screamed Mr. Peacock.

Only in answer to your screaming, screamed Mrs. Shoutington.

If I promise not to scream will you promise not to scream? screamed Mr. Peacock.

Yes, screamed Mrs. Shoutington.

Very well, then, said Mr. Peacock.

I hope, Mr. Kneesock, you will not forget that I am a woman of the upper-class, said Mrs. Shoutington.

That's exactly why I wanted to confer with you. I can get nothing from the servants. The Captain of Police is just as bad. Of course he's a person on the same level as the servants, said Mr. Peacock.

He's a very attractive man, I wonder if you've noticed? Perhaps it's the uniform? said Mrs. Shoutington.

I do wish you would understand that I do not discuss the physical aspects of servants and politicians. They are no more remarkable than, say, an ox in a field. They are paid to perform certain duties. But they are not to be considered people in the sense, say, that I am, said Mr. Peacock.

You're quite right, especially the Maid. She's built exactly like an ox. I'm quite sure you've noticed the difference in our figures, Mr. Wetfrock, said Mrs. Shoutington.

I do wish you would change the subject, cried Mr. Peacock.

What do you mean? said Mrs. Shoutington.

— 2 3 —

I mean the Maid's figure, screamed Mr. Peacock.

Why are you screaming? screamed Mrs. Shoutington.

Because I am getting sick of your endless discussion of the Maid's figure, screamed Mr. Peacock.

I'm sure she does quite well without your defending her, yelled Mrs. Shoutington.

I'm not defending her. I don't give a damn about her, screamed Mr. Peacock.

Don't hide it, Mr. Peahen, I was a married woman. I understand these things, said Mrs. Shoutington.

Are you trying to drive me out of my mind? Are you a conspirator with the Maid and the Caretaker? I wouldn't doubt that the Captain of Police is in it with you, cried Mr. Peacock.

In what? What are you talking about? cried Mrs. Shoutington.

My chair! Won't anybody listen to me? screamed Mr. Peacock.

Not if you're going to shout, shouted Mrs. Shoutington.

I'm trying to find out what you know about the chair's disappearance, said Mr. Peacock.

Do you think I have a nice figure? said Mrs. Shoutington.

Aren't you tired of displaying yourself like a woman of the streets? yelled Mr. Peacock.

I just don't understand you. You invite me over here, and then you begin to insult me, said Mrs. Shoutington.

I asked you over here because I felt you were a woman of breeding and sensitivity. The rest have been driving me crazy. And now you come here to drive me out of my mind. Why do you want to hurt me, Mrs. Shoutington? said Mr. Peacock.

I don't want to hurt you, Mr. Petcock. You see, we live quiet lives here. Sitting in the evenings, talking quietly and sipping brandy before the fire . . ., said Mrs. Shoutington.

That's what the servants do. Do you sit with them drinking up my brandy? screamed Mr. Peacock.

I have been a guest here. I have been entertained by the Maid and the Caretaker after old Mr. Sickcock became too ill to entertain. I see nothing wrong with servants taking over some of the responsibilities of the master. What are servants for? said Mrs. Shoutington.

Do you mean you would actually sit with servants and sip brandy with them? yelled Mr. Peacock.

Well, Mr. High-&-Mighty, it's a lot less of a thing than your affair with the Maid, said Mrs. Shoutington.

I thought I made it clear that I just met the Maid today, and that I find her socially completely inferior, screamed Mr. Peacock.

Ho ho, Mr. Horsecock, I think I am sufficiently grown-up to understand these things, said Mrs. Shoutington.

Shut up, shut up, screamed Mr. Peacock.

Oh, don't act so childish. You act just like a child who needs a physic, said Mrs. Shoutington.

How dare you call me a child, and make personal reference to my biological condition? roared Mr. Peacock.

There there, I was only fooling, said Mrs. Shoutington.

I know, but sometimes I feel so unsure of myself . . . And when a woman laughs at me . . . , whimpered Mr. Peacock.

I think we can be friends, Mr. Limpcock, said Mrs. Shoutington.

I hope so. And you do have a better figure than the Maid, said Mr. Peacock.

Oh, do you really think so? cried Mrs. Shoutington.

Yes, I do, said Mr. Peacock.

Oh, I'm so glad. Look at me now, said Mrs. Shoutington.

But, about the chair . . . , said Mr. Peacock.

Do you really think my figure is better than the Maid's? said Mrs. Shoutington.

Yes! Yes! Yes! How many times must I say yes? I'm sick of your figure, screamed Mr. Peacock.

Oh, I suppose you like the Maid's better? yelled Mrs. Shoutington.

I don't like yours and I don't like the Maid's. And I don't like the Caretaker's. I am interested in one thing, the chair, screamed Mr. Peacock.

All right, I'll talk about your chair if that's all you want to talk about, said Mrs. Shoutington.

What do you know about it, Mrs. Shoutington? said Mr. Peacock.

Well, as you know, I have been a frequent guest of the Maid and the Caretaker, as well as old Mr. Limpcock, said Mrs. Shoutington.

Why did you put my relative last, as if the servants owned the house? said Mr. Peacock.

Oh, does it sound like that? Well, I must admit that I saw a lot more of them than I did of the old Peafowl, said Mrs. Shoutington.

He was dying then, wasn't he? said Mr. Peacock.

Even before he was dying they had him working in the kitchen. Sometimes they'd let him serve the drinks, said Mrs. Shoutington.

Serve the drinks? Work in the kitchen? screamed Mr. Peacock.

Oh, yes, old Mr. Pighock did his best to please, until he got too sick, said Mrs. Shoutington.

You mean the servants took over? said Mr. Peacock.

I wouldn't say that. They were all like a family. The Maid and the Caretaker, the parents, and the old Peafowl, their child, said Mrs. Shoutington.

I see, said Mr. Peacock.

I never once saw the Caretaker strike old Mr. Sickcock, said Mrs. Shoutington.

How nice of the Caretaker not to strike his master, screamed Mr. Peacock.

Oh yes, they both treated him like their own child, said Mrs. Shoutington.

And the chair, Mrs. Shoutington? said Mr. Peacock.

The chair was old Mr. Petcock's. Not just a simple possession, but more like a dog. The chair liked him. You could almost see the chair moving to the part of the room where he was, said Mrs. Shoutington.

How strange, said Mr. Peacock.

Not that old Mr. Alarmclock neglected to notice my figure; the cut of my rump, said Mrs. Shoutington.

Is it possible that the servants, because of the elder Peacock's special interest, came to place a high value on this particular chair in their animal ignorance? And when they saw their chance, stole it? said Mr. Peacock.

Oh, I don't think so. They preferred the sofas and stuffed chairs. They were always sitting on the more comfortable furniture. They seemed to have an eye for comfort, said Mrs. Shoutington.

Perhaps they were merely hiding their greed? Servants are shrewd, like animals. They wait for the right moment to pounce, said Mr. Peacock.

I must say, Mr. Praecox, you seem somewhat unbalanced. The chair was of little value. It was a common wooden chair covered with chipped paint, said Mrs. Shoutington.

Unbalanced? Unbalanced because I want to keep my estate complete? Don't you see that this is only the beginning? The chair's theft provides the drain-hole for the rest of my goods, screamed Mr. Peacock.

But life goes on, Mr. Flintlock. How long do you think I will continue to have this beautiful figure? said Mrs. Shoutington.

I don't want to hear about your figure. I don't think your figure is particularly outstanding, screamed Mr. Peacock.

It's better than the Maid's, shouted Mrs. Shoutington.

The Maid, the Maid! Why do you keep comparing yourself to a serving woman? Anybody has a better figure than a serving woman. Look at my figure, for instance. You can see perfect evidence of the fine food, the refined posture of mind, and all the other things that contribute to the nobility of the flesh, roared Mr. Peacock.

I don't like your figure, Mr. Pighock. For one thing, you are too fat. The Caretaker, though much your senior, displays a keener biology than you, said Mrs. Shoutington.

The Caretaker? Why, he's a bent old man, stingy-fleshed and wrinkled. And besides, how dare you compare me with a servant? Do you think I'm in competition with that thief? screamed Mr. Peacock.

## THE ARRANGEMENTS

The Maid and the Caretaker are both far wealthier than you. Perhaps you don't know it, but old Mr. Flintlock left them all his money, said Mrs. Shoutington.

What is this you are saying? screamed Mr. Peacock.

Yes, I was at the reading of the will. The money went to the servants for their kind and reasonable treatment of him. The house went to you. Didn't you receive the papers? said Mrs. Shoutington.

Yes, but I assumed that I got everything. I don't read legal documents; that's for bureaucrats, screamed Mr. Peacock.

Old Mr. Peafowl thought it would be nice if you and the servants lived here together, said Mrs. Shoutington.

What are you saying? That I would sit in the evening sipping brandy with servants? Comparing your figure with the Maid's until I was half crazy? screamed Mr. Peacock.

Your relative was a very intelligent man. He felt that if you had the house and the servants had the money, all three of you would live like a family, because you would need each other, said Mrs. Shoutington.

All right, all right, they can live here and pay the bills. But I will not sit with them in the evening sipping brandy. I will retire early, screamed Mr. Peacock.

But if you are not nice to the servants, why should they stay and pay the bills? said Mrs. Shoutington.

I don't know, I don't know. But they must, cried Mr. Peacock.

Where are they now, Mr. Petcock? said Mrs. Shoutington.

They're in jail, cried Mr. Peacock.

Oh, that's a very bad beginning, said Mrs. Shoutington.

But they didn't tell me they were rich. That would have made all the difference, cried Mr. Peacock.

They don't want to be loved because they are rich. They want to be loved only because you love them. Just because the Maid's figure isn't as good as mine doesn't mean you have to reject her completely, said Mrs. Shoutington.

I didn't reject her because of her figure. I rejected her because she's a servant; a low-class servant, deserving only contempt, screamed Mr. Peacock.

Are you sure it wasn't her figure? said Mrs. Shoutington.

Why are you so physical? screamed Mr. Peacock.

It's you who is physical. You keep looking at people's figures, as if they could help looking the way they do. Have you no charity? shouted Mrs. Shoutington.

I don't care what people look like. If they are rich they are naturally good-looking. If they are poor they have no looks; not anymore than an animal of the fields, cried Mr. Peacock.

Now that you know the Maid is rich you'll probably think she has a better figure than mine, said Mrs. Shoutington.

She's still a servant. Money alone doesn't make a person rich, screamed Mr. Peacock.

If you'll only look at my figure Mr. Peacock, said Mrs. Shoutington.

Please, not at a time like this. Can't you see that I'm in crisis? screamed Mr. Peacock.

You have only to go to the police station and apologize to the servants, Mr. Petcock.

I can't apologize to inferiors, yelled Mr. Peacock.

But they're rich, said Mrs. Shoutington.

That's right. That gives me full right to go down on my knees and beg them to come back. I can even kiss their feet as a further act of repentance, cried Mr. Peacock.

You can even pretend to admire the Maid's figure. Although, just between us, it's greatly inferior to mine, said Mrs. Shoutigton.

Oh, damn your figure, screamed Mr. Peacock.

Oh, so now that the Maid is rich you like her figure better than mine, said Mrs. Shoutington.

Please, I'm trying to think of how to humiliate myself in front of the servants, and you keep on with your sex talk. I don't like sex. It is dirty and disgusting. The body is merely a medium for carrying clothes, and to provide a place for the neck to root, that it might hold up the head, screamed Mr. Peacock.

Sex? shouted Mrs. Shoutington.

It's for people who get all excited about the morbid aspects of the body. Weaklings and degenerates. The filthy-minded who crave unnatural encounters with unlikely places of the body. Enough of your emotional nonsense, Mrs. Shoutington! cried Mr. Peacock.

# The Return of the
# Peacock Servants

THE MAID AND THE CARETAKER stood in the
doorway . . .

You may enter. But do not think that any of the disciplinary
attitudes that I have expressed before have been relaxed, said Mr.
Peacock.

It's good to be home, said the Maid.

That's a very human attitude. But please remember that this is
my home, and I will tolerate very little as regards your behavior,
said Mr. Peacock.

What about him? said the Caretaker.

THE SONG OF PERCIVAL PEACOCK

Him? What him? Who? What? There are two hims in this room. What him are you referring to? Or are you talking about church music? yelled Mr. Peacock.

Him, sir. The other one, said the Caretaker.

He means the Peacock Dwarf, said the Maid.

What is all this? What are you saying in your animal mutterings? cried Mr. Peacock.

We're saying that you have yet to present yourself to the Dwarf, said the Maid.

What is this you are saying? cried Mr. Peacock.

Old Mr. Sickcock's son, said the Maid.

Son? screamed Mr. Peacock.

Shhh, it's a secret, said the Maid.

Stop shshing me and tell me who this person is, screamed Mr. Peacock.

It's his house, too. He's old Mr. Pisscock's son, said the Maid.

I'm the only relative that the elder Peacock had, yelled Mr. Peacock.

You're his nephew, ain't you? said the Maid.

I'm something or other, which is none of your business, screamed Mr. Peacock.

Well, the Dwarf's his son, said the Maid.

But the house was left to me, cried Mr. Peacock.

But the Dwarf has full rights, said the Maid.

Full rights? cried Mr. Peacock.

It's right in the will, said the Maid.

I don't read legal instruments. They're written by inferior minds, said Mr. Peacock.

You see, Mr. Prettycock, as much as we like you, we take our orders from the Dwarf, said the Caretaker.

I hope you won't make the Dwarf angry, said the Maid.

Make him angry. He better be sure that he doesn't make me angry, screamed Mr. Peacock.

You wouldn't fight with your cousin, would you, Mr. Peacock? said the Maid.

Cousin? He's no cousin of mine, cried Mr. Peacock.

Just because he's illegitimate doesn't mean he's not human, said the Maid.

Illegitimate, huh? That's why he didn't get the house, cried Mr. Peacock.

But the will says he has full rights to live here and give orders to the servants, said the Caretaker.

We'll see about that . . . , said Mr. Peacock.


## DIGITS AND UNDERWEAR

Look at these hands, said the Maid.

I don't want to look at a serving woman's hands. Take them away from my face, screamed Mr. Peacock.

Mr. Sweetcock, look at my feet, said the Caretaker.

Put your shoes back on! I do not want to look at any part of your serving man's body, roared Mr. Peacock.

Well, if you look at her hands you could look at my feet, that's only fair, said the Caretaker.

Please, not now. Can't you see how busy I am trying to make sense out of the mutterings of my servants, cried Mr. Peacock.

But. . . , said the Caretaker.

Enough. Just when I'm trying to think, you start to display your unwholesome extremities. For what reason I cannot tell. Nor do I wish to inquire any further into the matter as to why I am suddenly approached to make appraisals of your digital organs, cried Mr. Peacock.

If you don't want to look at my hands, that's your decision, I'm sure, said the Maid.

Will you please stop these sudden outbursts of personalizing, cried Mr. Peacock.

I'm just trying to say, Mr. Diaperbox, that I have no intention of using these fine instruments in laundry water, particularly in connection with your underclothes, said the maid.

How dare you refer to my undergarments? cried Mr. Peacock.

And I want to say, sir, that I refuse to put my foots in the laundry tub to moosh your clothes clean. Particularly, as this fine woman put it, with your underpants, said the Caretaker.

I quite understand your natural aversion to my loincloth. However, to make mention of it is the height of disrespect; lending a personal tone that tends to be both embarrassing and insulting, said Mr. Peacock.

Would you like us to put you to bed now, Mr. Sleepycock? said the Maid.

No, I would not like you to put me to bed, nor do I even want you to suggest such a thing. Do I look like I need you to undress and bathe me? cried Mr. Peacock.

We do not wish to remark on your person, said the Maid.

That's very good. But you must understand that there are certain things that I do for myself. I do not permit others to view my undressed body. Which precludes those intimacies associated with the personal care and maintenance of my person, said Mr. Peacock.

Do you want us to bathe you with laundry soap? said the Maid.

I want to help, screamed the Caretaker.

Both of you, stand back! I thought I just got through telling you that I have no wish to expose my naked self to the exploratory eyes of servants. And how dare you suggest washing me with laundry soap! cried Mr. Peacock.

Because we thought we could wash out the Dwarf's underwear as we bathed you, said the Maid.

You want to give me a bath in the same water with the Dwarf's underwear? screamed Mr. Peacock.

What's wrong with that? said the Caretaker.

You mean you are willing to wash the Dwarf's underwear, but not mine? screamed Mr. Peacock.

What's wrong with that? said the Caretaker.

I don't know. But there is something very wrong with it. And I just can't understand why his underwear must be washed in the same water that I'm to be bathed in, said Mr. Peacock.

Why not? said the Caretaker.

I cannot think why not. But it isn't right, said Mr. Peacock.

You're overly tired, dear. Why don't you go right to bed without your bath? said the Maid.

All right, mommy, whimpered Mr. Peacock.

There there; now just get going. You are dismissed, said the Maid.

What do you mean I am dismissed? How dare you dismiss me from my own living room, mother? screamed Mr. Peacock.

Do what you want, said the Maid.

Don't you dare speak to me like that, screamed Mr. Peacock.

The Peacock Dwarf will take care of you, said the Maid.

My house is full of strange people, screamed Mr. Peacock.

Sir, you're the only stranger here, said the Caretaker.

I'm told in my own home that I am the stranger. Where then is there comfort in this lonely world? Where may a man lay his head in peace? cried Mr. Peacock.

Oh, go along with you, said the Maid.

I'm tired anyway, That's the only reason I'm going to bed, said Mr. Peacock.

Good night, dear, said the Caretaker.

Don't call me dear. It's an improper address to a grown man; too personal an address of the servant to his master, yawned Mr. Peacock.

Oh, go upstairs now, said the Maid.

I'm tired anyway, yawned Mr. Peacock.

# Peacock Spanked

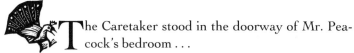The Caretaker stood in the doorway of Mr. Peacock's bedroom . . .

Oh, Mr. Bedrock, whispered the Caretaker.

Who is that? screamed Mr. Peacock.

It's me. The Maid asked me to get you up, whispered the Caretaker.

What time is it? screamed Mr. Peacock.

It's five in the morning, sir, said the Caretaker.

Five? How dare you wake me so early? screamed Mr. Peacock.

We couldn't sleep, so we thought we might as well wake you, said the Caretaker.

You mean that I am to be awakened every time you have insomnia? screamed Mr. Peacock.

No no, sir, I was really tired. It was the Dwarf who told us to get you up. No, I am really quite tired. Here, let me get in with you, said the Caretaker.

Get out of my bed, screamed Mr. Peacock.

Oh, it's so nice and warm, Mr. Sleepycock, said the Caretaker.

I do not want a servant to get into bed with me, yelled Mr. Peacock.

Oh, please, Mr. Beddycock, let's rest for an hour. I just love to get into bed with sleepy people, said the Caretaker.

You are a sexual deviate, screamed Mr. Peacock.

I liked you from the first moment I saw you, said the Caretaker.

It is not right for men to like other men, yawned Mr. Peacock.

Oh, I like people's bodies very much, Mr. Peepeecock. I would love to see your body, Mr. Pussycock. I would love to touch it, said the Caretaker.

I do not permit people to touch my body. The flesh is not only the house of the soul, but a vehicle, including intake ports as well as exhaust ports; not to mention areas given wholly to the reproductive cycle. These areas are of particular note. They grow more meaningfully terrible in direct ratio to one's growing sense of modesty, said Mr. Peacock.

Oh, Mr. Horsecock, I love it when you talk about the body. I get a hard-on, cried the Caretaker.

The flesh is merely a compromise to an environment. But we must be able to reduce it from a tantalizing sexuality by viewing it as a machine that functions beyond our sense of delicacy, said Mr. Peacock.

Oh, we must compromise, mustn't we, Mr. Weeweecock? cried the Caretaker.

We must not admit to compromising. We turn away blushing while our bodies commit us to terrible acts, yelled Mr. Peacock.

Oh, Mr. Freecock, it's utterly thrilling, cried the Caretaker.

Get out of my bed, screamed Mr. Peacock.

Not now, not after all the beautiful things you've said, cried the Caretaker.

Beautiful? I was merely explaining the difficulties, the immodesties of nature, the cruel joke of the function. I was pointing out the difficult ugliness that we are forced to wallow in, yelled Mr. Peacock.

Oh, but let's make the best of it, cried the Caretaker.

The best of it is that we recognize order . . . My dear Caretaker, it is most improper that you should be lounging in your master's bed, said Mr. Peacock.

Oh, but it's so warm and cozy. I just love your bed, cried the Caretaker.

Get out of my bed, screamed Mr. Peacock.

Oh, please, I will kiss your foots, cried the Caretaker.

You cannot bribe me with kisses. I am oblivious to sensual tribute, cried Mr. Peacock.

I will even let you kiss my foots, cried the Caretaker.

The prospect does offer, I must admit, some challenge to my sense of disgust; whether or no to override my natural nobility, and reach into the gutter, giving greater comparison to my loftier sensibilities . . . However, as usual, my impoverished emotional scale withholds the melody of longing that drives men to perverse pleasures. And I say again, get out of my bed, screamed Mr. Peacock.

Would you like a spanking? said the Caretaker.

A spanking? Do you dare entertain any cruel possibilities towards me? Do you really think I am to be handled like a child; a man closing nearly three hundred pounds, head of the Peacock estate? . . . A lowly servant is going to give such a man a spanking? screamed Mr. Peacock.

I only meant, sir, that if it should become your necessity to need the physical lesson from one, though a servant by trade, older, and therefore, by seniority the rightful administrator of the Maid's wishes, whimpered the Caretaker.

I'm warning you that any attempt to spank me shall be met by a most high grade physical effort. Which may result in injuries to both you and the Maid. For when injustice is done me, beware; I rise in all justice. But in my rage, fail, and carry justice to injustice, and put them who would treat me unjustly to even greater injustice, cried Mr. Peacock.

The Maid stood in the doorway of Mr. Peacock's bedroom and cried, get out of that bed, you monsters.

How long have you been standing there, you kitchen creature? screamed Mr. Peacock.

Long enough to know what the rich degenerate does with the poor serving man, cried the Maid.

A social revolution in my bedroom, screamed Mr. Peacock.

I suppose you think I haven't feelings? said the Maid.

No more so than the ox straining against a plow. The brute meditation that leads by nightfall to the dark uneventful barn, where the moon perhaps sends an arm of light to caress the brow of the brute. That head of dull eyes, and dunce hat horns . . . No no, it is an unfair circumstance that you view. Whereas I admit it has a sexual flavor, a proper investigation would reverse your conclusion. The Caretaker, drawn to the warmth that my body sheds like a serpent's skin, got into bed with me. And after some remarks having been passed between us, the Caretaker thought a spanking would be most appropriate. I then reviewed the difficulties to be encountered should he move punitively against my person. So you see, whatever sexuality might have been implied by our proximity, quite the reverse obtains, said Mr. Peacock.

Still, it isn't right for the master to force the man servant, said the Maid.

I have tried to explain to you, since I do feel that morality cuts across lines of class. However, you refuse to understand, and repeat the same allegations. So I don't care what you believe. And I ask both of you to leave my bedroom immediately, screamed Mr. Peacock.

You needn't raise your voice to me, Mr. Horsecock. I am not be forced by fear of dismissal like the Caretaker. For though I am your servant, I am still a person with sufficient auditory gift not to need the cruel stimulation of your scream, said the Maid.

Get out, get out, or I'll choke you to death, screamed Mr. Peacock.

You are yet due for a spanking, Mr. Badcock. Your threats are needless and foolish in the face of your oncoming spanking; to which you have been building toward since your arrival here. We know quite well how to handle the young gentlemen, said the Maid.

Get out of my room before I kill myself, screamed Mr. Peacock.

I'm afraid I'll have to spank you, sir, whimpered the Caretaker. Just try it, screamed Mr. Peacock.

You are too defiant, and should be slapped across the face, said the Maid.

Gaining up, huh? Okay, I'll take on the two of you, cried Mr. Peacock.

Just lie across my lap, Mr. Naughtycock, and I'll tan your hide, whimpered the Caretaker.

Do you really think I shall willingly lie across your bony lap with my sitting organ laid bare for your unauthorized judgment expressed in pain, as if I were a child with no say in the use of my body? Oh, no, you will find me a full grown man, with the accompanying strength of the mature Homo sapiens. And I will fight you if you dare the humiliation of myself in front of the Maid by exposing my sitting organ; insulting it by beating it with a hairbrush, cried Mr. Peacock.

No! No! I will beat your head with a hammer. And whilst punishing you, still, I shall be putting you to the kindness of unconsciousness, whimpered the Caretaker.

What are you saying? Can you really believe that I will submit to any kind of injurious treatment at your hands? I shall choke you to death. Put that hammer down! screamed Mr. Peacock . . .

# The Peacock Mother

AFTER SEVERAL DAYS   Mr. Peacock suddenly stood in the doorway of consciousness and screamed, he hit me on the head with a hammer!

A terrible blow delivered to a small area, said the Maid.

The simple description implied in the accusation of having been struck on the head with a hammer is sufficiently forceful, without the insult of the servant describing the act with technical objectivity, removing it from the sphere of moral consideration, screamed Mr. Peacock.

A terrible blow delivered to a small area has not only the weight of the hammer's head driven by the bony arm of the Caretaker, but also contains the weight of the many spankings put off in service to the hope of your changing. Therefore, in the cruelty of the blow is also morality justified, said the Maid.

What makes you think that I am unaware of the proper address of the servant to her master? Which is to be as brief as possible, conveying as much information in the shortest possible time. However, you take these occasions of intercourse for lengthy, convoluted, ill-phrased orations; which are aimed at my educated background, to prove that the shrewdness of the servant is equal to the university education of the master. But never does your ignorance shine forth more brightly than when you attempt to clothe it in educated phraseology. And, as to the notion of spanking a man well into his forties, his earning many spankings put off, only to be compounded in a single hammer's blow, that this is morally justified . . . , said Mr. Peacock.

Yes it is, yes it is, screamed the Maid.

It is not. It is not. There is no code on earth to justify such extreme action in the face of the allegations made against my conduct. Only in the most hideous phases of history are any such practices recorded, screamed Mr. Peacock.

You asked for it, screamed the Maid.

I asked to be hit on the head with a hammer? Are you out of your senses? screamed Mr. Peacock.

We acted in the child's best interests, cried the Maid.

Please, this whole conversation turns my stomach, said Mr. Peacock.

You haven't once complimented my figure, said the Maid.

You are no more to be noticed than an ox in a field. And you had better not start that business again, cried Mr. Peacock.

You might have lied, if only out of love. Some boys tell their mothers that their mothers are their best girls. Not you. No, Mr. Uppity wants his mother to crawl to him for compliments, said the Maid.

You are not my mother. And you are not worthy of compliments, screamed Mr. Peacock.

I suppose you think Mrs. Shoutington has a better figure than I do? You're very disloyal. But I suppose this is the price one pays for being such a devoted mother. You take me for granted; the old girl doesn't need any bouquets, said the Maid.

This has gone far enough. You dishonor the memory of my mother by attempting to steal her identity. How dare you insult your employer by dishonoring his mother, that beautiful woman of high attainment in both art and science? cried Mr. Peacock.

You are earning a spanking much faster than you know, my dear sir, said the Maid.

We are coming rapidly to my having to put you out on the road with nothing but a paper bag full of apples, unless you are willing to go down on your knees and kiss my feet as token of humble servitude to my whim. Only this shall I accept, your abject humility as a salute of respect, said Mr. Peacock.

I hardly think the mother crawling to her son's foot promotes a proper relationship. If I were not your mother, but a younger woman, I might be driven to such an act by your imperiousness to prove my complete abandonment of all self-interest to your whim in my love of you. Which, in that case, would be of an intense sexual nature. But to begin such a road is to put us in grave danger of moral chaos, said the Maid.

Do you really believe, mother or no, I could be drawn into a sexual adventure with you? But should there be the slightest tingling of such a feeling, you constitute the least of stimulants, cried Mr. Peacock.

Are you saying that your mother is not pretty? cried the Maid.

I am saying that you have no more effect on me than an ox browsing on poison ivy, cried Mr. Peacock.

Enough of this conversation. You are too much the child, said the Maid.

Are you cutting the conversation off? screamed Mr. Peacock.

I believe that further talk only brings us closer to your next spanking, said the Maid.

## DISCOVERY AND THREAT

Where are my clothes? cried Mr. Peacock.

They got ruined. You went to the bathroom on yourself. Which, I might add, brought grave doubts to our minds as to your maturity. And then, in trying to restore your clothes to their former condition . . . , said the Maid.

Get to it, you long-winded prostitute, screamed Mr. Peacock.

Well, they shrunk-up. And when the Dwarf tried to stretch them they got shredded, said the Maid.

Shredded? But they're the only clothes I have, screamed Mr. Peacock.

Here's an old dress of mine, said the Maid.

I can't wear a woman's dress. It'll create the wrong impression, screamed Mr. Peacock.

Your father's clothes are too small for you. And the Dwarf, seeing what you did to your own clothes, absolutely refuses to lend you anything. So you'll just have to have a stiff upper lip and put my dress on, said the Maid.

I will not. And how dare you imply that I excreted on myself, screamed Mr. Peacock.

You most certainly did befoul your clothes. Like an infant. I cleaned you myself. Your father couldn't stand it. That kind of work always falls to the woman, said the Maid.

Are you implying that I was handled like an infant by you? Exposed before you without dignity? When? screamed Mr. Peacock.

When you were unconscious. I couldn't let you lie in your own exhausts, could I? And besides, it offered us, your father and the Dwarf, an opportunity to view you for further use, said the Maid.

Further use? screamed Mr. Peacock.

The use being, that should you get out of line, we have only to remind you that we have viewed you in what might be said, a most unflattering way, said the Maid.

I will choke you to death, you inhuman slops woman, screamed Mr. Peacock.

You have nothing to fear, we won't tell outsiders, said the Maid.

Outsiders? Tell outsiders what? screamed Mr. Peacock.

I'm sure you wouldn't want me to go into that, would you Mr. Horsecock? said the Maid.

I will choke you to death. I will blind you so that none shall believe what you know by optical means, screamed Mr. Peacock.

You would have to blind your father, the Dwarf, the Attic Wizard, the Cellar Maid, Mrs. Shoutington, not to mention the Captain of Police . . . , said the Maid.

Shut up. Shut up, screamed Mr. Peacock.

Believe it or not, Mrs. Shoutington thought you rather attractive. However, the Captain of Police said, rather candidly, that in his opinion you would bear watching in future. We asked him why. He replied that your genital development was rather precocious, said the Maid.

But I'm forty years old. How dare he make remarks concerning my excretory instrumentalities? screamed Mr. Peacock.

You might as well know that your father and I will not permit any sexual adventuring by you. This is part of the reason why we want you to wear a dress. You are capable of looking quite feminine. Besides, we had always hoped to have a daughter. We don't think your substituting will be too much of a burden. And your wearing a dress will advertise to the world that you are sexually a total waste of time, said the Maid.

But you are presuming an excretory instinct in me, which, in spite of my physical development, does not exist, cried Mr. Peacock.

I followed the professional advice of the Captain . . . Nor were the views expressed by Mrs. Shoutington an encouragement to allowing you to proceed further in your particular sexual bent, said the Maid.

But I tell you there is not the slightest chance that I shall go astray. For I loathe and detest all matters relating to the excretory functions, screamed Mr. Peacock.

But since we are not sure about your proclivity for lying, we must assume the responsibility to keep you from raping someone, said the Maid.

But I assure you, even the thought of touching another person's hand fills me with such repulsion that I shake with nausea, cried Mr. Peacock.

Why don't you leave these matters to us? After all, we love you, we wouldn't do anything to hurt you, said the Maid.

But I will decide for myself. I will choose my own restraints. How dare you, a lowly servant, suggest that I might commit some hideous crime, which the very thought of turns my stomach? screamed Mr. Peacock.


## THE HEIRLOOM

We have taken the further precaution of fitting you with a chastity belt, said the Maid.

Is that what this terrible iron affair is? said Mr. Peacock.

Yes. It's been in the family for centuries. We would by all means keep you from ending in a prison. We had the Captain of Police put it on you. He's very good with locks, said the Maid.

I am most distressed that you took all this upon yourself. You've obviously gone to a great deal of trouble on my behalf. But I assure you, my very skull is a chastity belt, and that I have no need for this secondary safety factor in the name of chastity. I thank you very much for your thoughtful and considerate concern for my well-being. But as for wearing a chastity belt and a woman's dress to ward off possible romantic interludes, nothing could be more foreign to my tastes. So that this apparatus merely constitutes an unhygienic nuisance, said Mr. Peacock.

We didn't think so. And, after all, we are the responsible ones, aren't we? said the Maid.

You most certainly are not. I can understand, and even applaud your solicitous concern for your master. But when you become insistent that you are right above the judgment of your master, you jump the track into impudence. And, where I would wish to employ disciplinary action, not so much for your intent, which I have said is laudable; but after having been proven wrong, your insistence, even at the expense of your master's comfort, said Mr. Peacock.

In the case where your judgment versus ours, we must then disregard yours, because we are older. And, whereas time may prove us wrong, we should be more than foolhardy to allow important matters to be decided by a mere child; who even now shows rebelliousness . . . And with his precocious genital development, the signs become too evident that a dangerous situation is developing. We would be less than loving if we allowed you to blunder, innocently enough, I grant you, into raping someone, said the Maid.

But I must remind you that you are not my parents; however flattering it might be to an employer that his servants take a parental interest in him. Still, as to his sexual potentialities, these matters I would think, in the name of taste and just simple respect, should be left up to the employer. It is not a pleasant thing, I assure you, to wake up after being hit on the head with a hammer, locked in a chastity belt. Which, though charming enough for its cunning locks . . . Rather like a bird's cage, isn't it? Still, it seems to me rather high-handed of servants to fit the master with such a device. Not the least of it, that servants take this opportunity to view the master's excretory instrumentalities; even to bringing in the police to help with the fitting, that the master's instrumentalities might come to remark in the repertory of the Captain of Police, said Mr. Peacock.


A QUESTION OF GENDER


We could not rightly take it upon ourselves to predict the safety of the community; so that our calling the police in to give expert testimony was ordered by necessity rather than just his curiosity. Of course he was curious. That's only natural when it comes to viewing a nude person. At first he suggested a gray, female prisoner's dress. But they're so drab that I immediately rejected that for you. I knew you would prefer a nice flower design. Why should I not dress you as prettily as I would have dressed my daughter, had I had a daughter? said the Maid.

I quite understand your rejecting the drab prison dress for me. And applaud you again for your solicitous concern. But, as for wearing a dress, I see little reason to invite speculation as to my gender. Most people take me to be male. And, whereas I do not further identify myself by any activities with the opposite gender, my name is Percival, which seems to demand male clothes to further the effect started by my name. A name I believe reserved only for males, said Mr. Peacock.

That would be very easily solved by merely putting a sign on the back of your dress. It could read, I am male, but sexually dangerous, said the Maid.

Well, whereas the sign would offer the opportunity to establish my gender, which is always useful when exact description is called for. Yet, the sexually dangerous part would only tend to disfigure my social stance. It would imply that I am voluntarily holding myself up to public pity by so declaring my lack of bathroom training, said Mr. Peacock.

Perhaps you shall inspire pity. But then the tide shall turn, and in pity's place shall come a tide of grateful thanks. That you took it upon yourself at the loss, I might add, of quite some social prestige in the beginning to warn the populace of the danger indigenous to your freakism, said the Maid.

No, I refuse, no matter how nice it would be to receive many heartfelt thanks. No, it is simply out of the question for a man of my social rank to seek popular approval; that vulgar twentieth century desire for generalized love. Which men of my stature must despise out of hand, cried Mr. Peacock.

Don't you want to go among people? Garden Parties? PTA meetings? said the Maid.

Do you really think I could enjoy mixing with people while wearing a sign on my back advertising my lack of bathroom training? Do you think that any pleasure could arise in me by appear-

ing in an old woman's dress? Smiling all the while, hoping no one
is noticing the tears unavoidably running down my cheeks. And
always that hideous sign on my back. I even wonder if such a sign
wouldn't provoke laughter rather than gratitude? said Mr. Peacock.

I shall introduce you as my daughter, said the Maid.

I am not your daughter, screamed Mr. Peacock.

I shall say to everyone, attention, attention, please, this is my
daughter, said the Maid.

But I am not a girl. This dress is merely an expedient measure
used to avert an unpleasant prediction, screamed Mr. Peacock.

Well, I can't introduce you as my son, said the Maid.

I am not your son, screamed Mr. Peacock.

What I mean to say is, that if I introduced you as my son, and
you were wearing that dress, it would seem to the populace that
you were one of those homosexual types who enjoy disguising as
old women. It would be too embarrassing. Of course the measures
we have taken for controlling your unnatural proclivity presents
many drawbacks. However, the alternatives are even more dev-
astating, said the Maid.

I will have none of it. Because I have been tolerant toward your
views on the matter, and have listened with an open mind, does
not mean that I have agreed with your hideous conclusions. I am
in no way dangerous, except perhaps to you. For I feel like chok-
ing you to death. You are forgetting your position. Your constant
reference to me as your offspring is most offensive. And your
remedies for a supposed affliction of mine are, to say the least,
most hideous. Not to mention the very affliction, which implies a
function which I am completely lacking in, cried Mr. Peacock.

All that you say has some merit, I admit this. You are not totally
lacking in judgment. No son of mine could be. However, it must
be remembered that it is the parental duty to safeguard the child
from self-injury. This is the practical side of love. And takes the
form very often of disciplinary action, such as a spanking or a fist
to the jaw, should the situation warrant such measures. You will
do as your father and I command, or you shall be punished. We

shall always be willing to consider your suggestions as to your proper management. However, we shall be the final judges as to the appropriate actions to be taken in your management, said the Maid.

## A STRATEGY

I see . . . And how does this apply to the missing chair? said Mr. Peacock.

Well, if we've gotten you settled we might go into that, said the Maid.

I believe the whole difficulty here might hinge directly on the chair; the theft involved in its loss . . . I believe if we worked together in solving this crime, assuming that you and the Caretaker are completely without guilt, we might arrive at an equitable solution to the many problems that have arisen, said Mr. Peacock.

I see what you mean. That by bypassing the known difficulties, and approaching them from the other way, by means of attacking a new problem, we might then, by viewing all past difficulties from this new direction, suddenly see them in their true light, said the Maid.

Well, that is a way of saying something, I believe. However, my true interest being the whereabouts of the missing chair, I might be willing to agree to any formula presented by you, whether or not I fully understand what you mean; not to mention even your intention, which may very well be a subtle root to further mischief against my person. Even so, if I keep my wits about me, and my ears open, I might just gain a word or two, which might be the keys that open a whole field, as it were, of possibilities, wherein the final clue will come to view. I might, by careful attention to your whims and delusions, gain that key to your guilt; that I might then be able to present a complete index of your guilt to the proper authorities . . . Gaining me some little reputation, by the way, as a detective. Then none shall say that one such as I should be the one to wear such things as a chastity belt and an old woman's dress;

not to mention old women's underwear . . ., said Mr. Peacock.

Yes, your summation is most impressive. And I look upon it, in spite of its many faults, with some matronly pride. However, if I understand correctly, you shall be willing to comply with our wishes in the management of yourself, even if the reasons you give for so complying run counter to the highest motives. Therefore, I feel free to indulge your curiosity concerning the chair; which, as you know, was a common piece of furniture, said the Maid.

Get on with it, cried Mr. Peacock.

As you realize, I am not a well woman, and have taken to developing various remedies to ease my suffering. The most notable treatment involving the use of mayonnaise rubbed generously over my body. This involves the complete dismissal of my clothes, which has inspired much vulgarity . . . The elder Peafowl, my father-in-law, who would take these occasions to view me through the kitchen window. Not to mention the Caretaker, who by this excuse and that excuse, found ways to position himself in the kitchen just as the most revealing part of my preparation was taking place; seeking view of my vulva at all times, said the Maid.

Spare me these hideous details, and get on with the materials concerning the missing chair, cried Mr. Peacock.


## THE DECOY

I'm trying to pick up the threads of the story as best as I can. The particular chair you are interested in just happens to be the chair I would put my clothes on. I have an excellent figure, I think, but this is no reason that my privacy should be invaded. However, to return to the chair. Being one who is fastidious with her clothes, I am perhaps overly protective as to their maintenance. As I removed them I would, in a sense, dress the chair, keeping each part of my costume in its relative position as regards my figure. What do you think of my figure? said the Maid.

It signifies as much to me as an ox seen in a distant field, cried Mr. Peacock.

I suppose you go more for the shrivelly-fleshed Mrs. Shout-ington? However, as I was saying, the chair in question became in some ways an effigy of myself. I would slip its hind legs into my underpants, strap my brassiere around its back; put its legs into my shoes, and so forth. I confess that after a while I even used the chair as a sort of decoy to draw the attentions of old Mr. Hardcock and the Caretaker away from me. Men are quite gullible, you know. Old Mr. Peepingcock was once seen on one knee before the chair, asking its hand in marriage. Quite seriously, what do you think of my figure? In all fairness, don't you think that in spite of my age and weight problem, it still has a great deal to say to the male libido? said the Maid.

Please have the decency not to indulge your fantasies in verbal form within my hearing. I find it most distressing to think that I have given you the impression that such confidences from a serv-ing woman are in any way welcome. If you have fallen into the tasteless habit of stripping where people can inadvertently view you, you must take full responsibility for the unwholesome events that follow on such ill-advised conduct. I, for one, should most certainly have avoided the kitchen had I known that such unsa-vory conditions existed there. All things pertaining to the repro-ductive cycle of human beings I find most tasteless, and highly charged with excretory thoughts. And I can't quite understand the interest shown by most people in these functions, when, if they should look about them there is so much that is more than worthy of mention. Beautiful sunsets, flowers and butterflies. . . , cried Mr. Peacock.


## VIRTUE

Surely you have not missed the fact that I am a woman of highest virtue, who has fallen, through no fault of her own, to conditions not fit for the lowest whore. But, owing to a terrible rheumatism, and lack of doctors willing to treat one without sensual payment, I am forced to minister to myself. Does not that chastity belt you are wearing not testify to my virtue? Surely you must view the belt with great admiration for me; seeing that so full of virtue am that it overflows to my son, said the Maid.

Yes yes, you are a woman of highest virtue. But I am hardly interested in the sordid details of a servant's life. Do you think I wish to spend my remaining days listening to testimony on the height your virtue has reached? I grow most weary at these continual admissions of immodesty. Only to be followed by lengthy reasons that lead to high praise of your virtue. You are, in fact, a most vulgar, stupid example of the working class. I would wish you would gain some objective view of yourself, that you might see how ridiculous your syntax is, screamed Mr. Peacock.

You are drawing conclusions simply by viewing an unfortunate situation not of my making . . . , said the Maid.

Enough, enough, I do not care what you do with your spare time. It is well known that servants are promiscuous. They are another class of domestic animal. They breed freely without benefit of marriage. Just another condition to be listed as one more of the ills of the world. However, if I might, I would like once more to get back to the chair, which is the reason for my attention. Surely you do not think I would allot this time and attention to you who are merely a lowly serving woman, were it not for the fact that I am most vitally interested in the chair, screamed Mr. Peacock.

Be that as it may, sir, events to have proper meaning must be set in their proper time relationships. For instance, of the time I am talking about, the chair was not missing. However, from that point on a time was reached, if for a second, when after it the chair began to be missing. If you see what I mean? said the Maid.

Of course, that is the nature of all change. It always happens in terms of space and time, cried Mr. Peacock.

So that to lose a portion of seemingly tedious detail is perhaps to lose an essential fact that might have led, perhaps, to the discovery of a new cure for rheumatism, said the Maid.

Rheumatism? screamed Mr. Peacock.

I mean a cure for the missing chair, which is like an illness; wouldn't you say? said the Maid.

An illness perhaps cured by a term in prison, cried Mr. Peacock.

How interesting. I wonder if that just wouldn't be worth trying for my rheumatism? Too many scientists pass up ideas which in the end are accidentally stumbled upon by a serving woman, said the Maid.

Shut up, or I'll choke you to death, screamed Mr. Peacock.

Why are you screaming at me? screamed the Maid.

Because you are trying me to the end of my restraint, screamed Mr. Peacock.

If you are not interested in my illness you have only to tell me. Surely you cannot think it is my wish to bore you with my personal difficulties? But you seemed to encourage a friendship, quite aside from the mother and son relationship; that I thought my dreams and concerns would be of interest to you, said the Maid.

I do not wish a friendship with servants. How can I ask you to clean up slops if our relationship has taken on a personal aspect? I ask no more of you than I would an animal. You are an animal that can talk and remember to some degree. I am merely making use of this faculty. I hope I haven't implied anything more than this? Now please confine yourself to a description of events leading to the disappearance of the chair, or I shall have to come to the conclusion again that you are indeed the cause of said disappearance. This can only lead to your re-arrest and my humiliation in having to beg you to return in lieu of my financial collapse; due to the faulty judgment of the elder Peacock in so foolishly leaving his money in your hands. Besides, I would loathe having to again come in contact with that hideous Captain of Police, who has, by your admission, viewed me in most unflattering conditions; and was, as you told me, the very one to lock me in this chastity belt. So please carefully choose your words. Come directly to the point of the missing chair. Or you shall set in motion this terrible machine that can only lead to my humiliation, screamed Mr. Peacock.

Your humiliation is mine, said the Maid.

## OF SERVANTS AND MASTERS

I do not ask servants to take on the ethical and moral penalties, not to say the emotional consequences of such penalties when in the time of the fall from grace. For that should raise them to unsubstantial balloon figures, hideous with noxious pride. Making of them grotesque confidants, which only compounds the moral and ethical shame, cried Mr. Peacock.

In the son's fall is also the mother's, said the Maid.

In the fall of the master is the spiteful giggle of malevolent servants, cried Mr. Peacock.

In a world of conspiratorial anger is the paranoid man awake in his own nightmare, said the Maid.

I will thank you to leave problems of psychological analysis to those trained by university standards. It is no more than the chirping monkey in a world of banana values that the servant brings forth wisdom, cried Mr. Peacock.

Do you really think I can spend the day trading educated guesses about your difficulty? I've the Dwarf's underwear to wash. I'll save the water for you, said the Maid.

That's another thing, I see no reason why the master should be asked to bathe in used laundry water. It rather makes the master feel he is worthy of less than his first thoughts on the subject would have led him to believe. But allowing that he should overcome this prohibition in his thoughts, he cannot let go of the idea that his servants have dared make this judgment of his worth. And in the self-acceptance of one's worth rises yet another emotion under the generalized heading of hate. Which, when brought to action is revenge on those who in the first instance had judged him through their own inferiority. Which must always see things as less than they. If I make myself clear? said Mr. Peacock.

As usual I haven't the faintest idea what you are talking about. And having no wish to be put through it again, must simply place it under the heading of just some more nonsense, said the Maid.

I am to be listened to; for, whereas your deficiency does not allow hope for your full emancipation from darkness, there is always the possibility of some small grains of wisdom rubbing off on you. And, as if this were not value enough, there is also the injunction upon you to treat your master with awe and respect until death us do part. And this is the first value which gains you the right to live, screamed Mr. Peacock.

Your jealousy is most unbecoming, said the Maid.

Jealousy? screamed Mr. Peacock.

You are obviously trying to keep your mother all for yourself. I know what you're about. You try to keep me talking all day instead of letting me wash the Dwarf's underwear, said the Maid.

You are on trial, madam. You stand before your judge. Do you think the judge cares about all the tedious vulgarities of the defendant? You are charged with the responsibility of the missing chair. You are being questioned, for the judge is not above kindness, he extends objective kindness unfettered with personal concerns, and allows you to present reasons why you should not be condemned, cried Mr. Peacock.

Although the Dwarf is not my son, still, in the association of the older woman and a younger person over a period of time, there grows that emotional thing which is equal, and perhaps in time more important than the biological tie associated with the maternal process. However, you are my son, and I do adhere to the cultural ideal of the mother and son contract. So that even if I should be emotionally remiss, still, I will live to the contract, and not neglect the necessary shows of maternal concern for you, said the Maid.

I do not ask more than simple obedience of the jumping servant to the master's whim, said Mr. Peacock.

That's very infantile, said the Maid.

I will thank you not to enter personal criticisms into our conversation, cried Mr. Peacock.

Will you just slip into your dress and come downstairs. I can't spend the whole day talking to you. You ought to have some friends. But you'd rather lie around all day in bed, said the Maid.

I ask you to stop talking to me in that tone, which indicates that we have been properly introduced. You shall leave when you have been dismissed, screamed Mr. Peacock.

I'm leaving. Your dress is laid out for you. Your chastity belt is locked, said the Maid.

But the chair, screamed Mr. Peacock.

Some other time, said the Maid.

Now, screamed Mr. Peacock.

# Peacock's Gruel

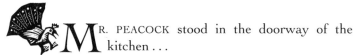M R. PEACOCK stood in the doorway of the kitchen . . .

You look just stunning, dear, cried the Caretaker.

Do not refer to me as dear, cried Mr. Peacock.

It was just an affectionate greeting for one's daughter, whimpered the Caretaker.

I am not your daughter. This dress represents only a poor substitute for the costume of my gender, cried Mr. Peacock.

But your mother said that you are now willing to be our daughter, whimpered the Caretaker.

I am not your offspring, screamed Mr. Peacock.

Well, I don't care; I, for one, think you have a lovely figure, said the Caretaker.

But I do not ask for your compliments, and find them an impertinence rather than a cause of celebration, cried Mr. Peacock.

Celebration? Of course! I shall sing and dance. I bet you didn't know your daddy could dance? cried the Caretaker.

You are not my daddy. And I will not have servants dancing. It tends to break down that important distance to be established between servant and master, instituted expressly for the purpose of . . . , screamed Mr. Peacock.

I just hope to God that your chastity belt is locked, shouted the Maid.

Did you dare to interrupt me? screamed Mr. Peacock.

Be quiet while I dish out your gruel, said the Maid.

Gruel instead of choice meats? Gruel instead of rare and softly blessed vegetables, overlaid with exquisite sauces? screamed Mr. Peacock.

Gruel made from watered oatmeal with a few cabbage leaves thrown in, said the Maid.

But I see lamb chops and artichokes, cried Mr. Peacock.

That's the Dwarf's dinner, said the Maid.

But, whereas I fully appreciate that the Dwarf does not fall below human consideration, I fail to see why such court is paid to his palate at the expense of the master's, who, through no fault of his, is given subhuman fare? said Mr. Peacock.

You're too fat. It's high time we brought you down to where intake is commensurate to expenditure, said the Maid.

I will not allow that a servant may make such a judgment; while, even so, there is some truth in your statement, as regards my external proportions, it is unfitting that the servant should make mention of it. It represents a breakdown in the caste system, cried Mr. Peacock.

Sweetheart, mother means that boys don't like fat girls, said the Caretaker.

I am not a girl. This dress is merely a substitute, worn only that my modesty be maintained. In better circumstances I should be wearing trousers, said Mr. Peacock.

Well, I don't care what anybody says, I think you look just sweet, said the Caretaker.

I have no wish to look sweet. A man takes this kind of a remark as an insult. And would you please stop touching me! At first I thought it was an accident. But you keep touching me in such a way that I can't help knowing the intent of your sensual appetite, screamed Mr. Peacock.

I was just straightening your dress, whimpered the Caretaker.

Keep your hands off my dress. Is it your habit to touch women's dresses? screamed Mr. Peacock.

But you're my daughter. Sexual intent would be the last thing that would animate my fingers, whimpered the Caretaker.

I said stop touching me, screamed Mr. Peacock.

I was merely straightening your dress, whimpered the Caretaker.

You have no right to put your hands on your employer, unless asked to . . . Which I assure you . . . Well, perhaps I might ask you to stoop and tie my shoe. But as to touching areas in the torso region, I assure you, this area is given over to too many excretory functions, screamed Mr. Peacock.

Do you think we want to hear about your illnesses at the supper table? I should hope you were brought up with a better sense of delicacy than to display your infirmities at the supper table, said the Maid.

I was merely explaining to the Caretaker that I do not want to be handled like some soliciting woman of the streets. And, that even if his purpose should be to my maintenance, rather than his sensual need, still, I find his hands, especially when they reach the torso area much too personal for me to remain quiet. I spoke at this time for I felt that any waiting on my part might then act the sign of permission and the complete dismissal on the Caretaker's part of all moral values to the excretory functions. And thereby involve me in what would seem a most spectacular loss of modesty, not to mention decency. Or to mention decency as the direct cause of my alarm. Not that I am capable of losing myself to such excretory delight. Which is the reason for my unusual strength in matters involving these involvements, said Mr. Peacock.

If you could possibly spare us these descriptions of your personal difficulties at the supper table we would be most grateful. After supper we can go to your room. I will listen to all your questions, and explain the female monthly cycle. You will find that growing up is not quite so frightening as it seems, said the Maid.

Will you keep your hands off me! screamed Mr. Peacock.

I was just fixing your skirt, whimpered the Caretaker.

Is that any way to talk to your father? said the Maid.

Your mother's right, said the Caretaker.

You are servants who, owing to reasons not fully understood, have taken on the obsession that you have produced a child in the name of Mr. Peacock. And though this is untrue, still I have been willing to live with this delusion for the sake of peace. However, when the so-called male parent who, under the impression that Mr. Peacock is his daughter, seeks out her excretory instrumentalities we are entering the illusionary world of incest, where no valid family texture remains, cried Mr. Peacock.

If the father loves his daughter, is that a crime? whimpered the Caretaker.

But, in fact, I am not your daughter. And so we enter into the world of homosexuality. These sexual worlds we keep entering are merely the results of poor bathroom training, said Mr. Peacock.

You don't see me wearing a chastity belt, whined the Caretaker.

How dare you impugn a legitimate course of moral instruction? screamed Mr. Peacock.

It is more restraint than instruction, whimpered the Caretaker.

This belt is not worn for punitive reasons, but rather as a prophylactic, cried Mr. Peacock.

So you won't get pregnant, whimpered the Caretaker.

It is a medicinal aid toward greater spiritual health. And does not speak to an existing difficulty, but rather speaks to a prophetic option read in my external conformations, screamed Mr. Peacock.

Excuses, excuses, you're wearing a chastity belt because we

fear that you might attract undue sexual attention, for which your father's advances provide fair evidence. I want to hear no more protestations to the otherwise, for you only add to your moral turpitude by becoming the liar, cried the Maid.

Your mother is right, you mustn't invite impure reactions in one old enough to be your father; and by strange coincidence, owing to the laws of biology, is your father . . . , whimpered the Caretaker.

You are but a servant making claim to high station by claiming fatherhood to a child of the ruling class . . . , said Mr. Peacock.

## SOMETHING *FUNNY*

Did you touch the Dwarf's plate? cried the Maid.

I didn't touch it, cried Mr. Peacock.

Didn't you touch his plate? screamed the Maid.

I said I didn't touch his plate, screamed Mr. Peacock.

I don't know, I just feel when my back is turned you're doing something funny, said the Maid.

I know perfectly well how to sit at a table without doing something funny, cried Mr. Peacock.

I caught you, screamed the Maid.

At what? screamed Mr. Peacock.

You were looking at my back. You were studying my figure, roared the Maid.

I was not. I was merely looking in your direction. Which is perfectly natural when one is engaged in conversation, cried Mr. Peacock.

You were trying to imagine me without clothes. Don't deny it. All you have on your mind is sex, screamed the Maid.

I swear to you that your physical presence affects me no more than the ox that browses in a distant field, cried Mr. Peacock.

I'm warning you, I know you're doing something funny. You're either touching the Dwarf's plate, or looking at me when my back is turned, roared the Maid.

I swear to you that whereas I feel a certain injustice in the Dwarf having lamb chops and artichokes, while I must be content with gruel, still, you cannot imagine that I would steal from his plate. The injustice of it becomes that much more cruel when you suggest that I would stoop to thievery when, should I have wished it, I could have demanded equal fare. But I bowed to you medical analysis of my figure, and allowed that gruel might be the very tonic that an essentially athletic figure, given over by certain worries and late illness to a softening, which might be described as a flabby situation, might respond to rising again to its former splendid achievements on the field of sport, said Mr. Peacock.

Just keep your hands out of his plate. You don't see him dipping into your plate, do you? said the Maid.

I have explained to you, that whereas your suspicions have an element of possibility, that resides mainly in the quality of cuisine, most tempting indeed, lamb chops and artichokes . . . Placed against gruel in a competition of savoriness, the lamb chops and artichokes must certainly win. However, to imply that I am recklessly given over to my impulses is to impugn my restraint in regard to the other vices. So that by your foregone conclusion you make me out to be sensually driven. For one who is not loth to steal from a supper plate is not likely to be dissuaded from intimate associations with the sexual instrumentalities, said Mr. Peacock.

Please, no more. I think you had better go to your room now, said the Maid.

I have done nothing, cried Mr. Peacock.

Nevermind, it's not your fault, said the Maid.

But you still believe I have done something, even if you do take a charitable attitude, cried Mr. Peacock.

Take what you can, you sneak. Be grateful I don't call the Captain of Police and have you arrested for tampering with the Dwarf's plate, screamed the Maid.

Be grateful that you don't call the Captain of Police? You should be kissing my feet with humble acceptance of my kingship in the realm of kindness and patience, screamed Mr. Peacock.

I refuse to indulge you in any of your proclivities, which are the reasons you wear a chastity belt. Go along with the Caretaker to your room, said the Maid.

I do not need any assistance, cried Mr. Peacock.

That chastity belt makes you a little bowlegged, and I insist that the Caretaker help adjust your heft on the stairway. Meanwhile, you can play little flower girl, said the Maid.

I am not a little girl. And I do not enjoy playing games designed to entertain little girls, screamed Mr. Peacock.

Come along, dear, said the Caretaker.

Do not call me dear. It is most unfitting that a stringy old man should address his master, a rather powerfully built athlete, as if he were a little girl, cried Mr. Peacock.

Come, sweetheart, said the Caretaker.

I asked you not to refer to me as if I were some small child, easily bribed by endearing terms to do your bidding. I am a grown man in the prime of his manhood. Perhaps somewhat overweight. But a little gruel will soon fix that . . . , said Mr. Peacock.

Good night, screamed the Maid.

# Peacock Visited by Mrs. Yellington

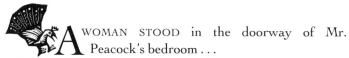A WOMAN STOOD in the doorway of Mr. Peacock's bedroom . . .

Who are you? screamed Mr. Peacock.

I have come for my rights, said the woman.

Rights? Who am I to give justice, when I too am a victim of injustice? cried Mr. Peacock.

Are you not the young Peacock? said the woman.

I am he, and as such, do demand certain protocol. You should have been announced. What right have you to invade my bedroom? screamed Mr. Peacock.

I do not like your servants, said the woman.

Oh, so you know them? Yes, you are quite right, they are most impossible. You seem a woman of the upper-class, and you did right to avoid them. In this case I shall waive my privacy in lieu of the comradeship I crave for one of my own class, said Mr. Peacock.

I think you misunderstand my visit. I am not one of those women who make themselves available for a price, said the woman.

How dare you think I am attempting a romantic adventure with you? I am completely without care for the sensual direction you imply, screamed Mr. Peacock.

I do not care to view you in the undress, sir. I find, after a very unfortunate series of events, that the difference which marks the man from the woman totally disgusting, yelled the woman.

If you imagine that I would be willing to pull my dress up and display the iron cage of my discipline where the bird of my displeasure lives, you are delirious in your heat. And I shall not by any persuasion be caught up in your necessity, cried Mr. Peacock.

I tell you, my need has turned to disgust. What was the loss of self in the need of another is now only nausea. If you approach me I shall vomit on you, yelled the woman.

I wish no contact with your excretory functions. I warn you that any such response from any part of your body shall be met with a severe indifference, cried Mr. Peacock.

Do not put your hands on me, sir, yelled the woman.

You cannot make me, screamed Mr. Peacock.

I shall vomit on you, yelled the woman.

Why are you yelling? yelled Mr. Peacock.

Because I'm in danger, yelled the woman.

I did not ask you here, cried Mr. Peacock.

But I was forced by necessity, said the woman.

Necessity? The necessity to view the athlete asleep; hoping to see what is to be seen as he turns in his sleep, his covers coming off? . . . , cried Mr. Peacock.

I beg you to be fair, whimpered the woman.

Neither threat nor promise moves me from the path of virtue, said Mr. Peacock.

## TESTICLES

I have come for justice, said the woman.

What justice? cried Mr. Peacock.

It is the testicles of the elder Peacock, said the woman.

Testicles? screamed Mr. Peacock.

The pourings of which do with the woman so beget . . . , said the woman.

What talk is that? cried Mr. Peacock.

Dwarves, yelled the woman.

Who are you? And what has all this to do with the missing chair? screamed Mr. Peacock.

I am Mrs. Yellington. Surely you've heard of me? yelled Mrs. Yellington.

And what of the missing chair? screamed Mr. Peacock.

That is a whole story, which is neither the burden nor the point of my mission, said Mrs. Yellington.

But you do know of the chair? said Mr. Peacock.

Yes. There was once a chair that lived, even as you and I, which had come to much favor in the master's eye. But alas, the chair fell in with wicked servants, and was lost to the ways of evil, said Mrs. Yellington.

At last I've found somebody who really knows about the chair, screamed Mr. Peacock.

What was at first a life of virtue turned now toward the shadows of corruption; and so sank down in darkness, said Mrs. Yellington.

Yes yes, very beautiful, but I want facts, screamed Mr. Peacock.

What was at first the bliss of an unforced virtue gave way to the slow pain of the quick pleasure; the lingering dark after the sensual lightning . . . , said Mrs. Yellington.

Yes yes, of course. But as to the chair, which is a material possession possessed by sentient beings, who create the evil in form of theft. I must beg you to get straight to the point, cried Mr. Peacock.

And so it was, where love had nurtured purity, the pollution of the evil heart o'erwhelmed and made ugly what God, in His first giving, had made in beauty . . . It brings tears to my eyes, whimpered Mrs. Yellington.

If you are trying to win my sympathy, which must lead in that softening to some sexual adventure, you are sadly mistaken, screamed Mr. Peacock.

You are missing the point, yelled Mrs. Yellington.

Missing the point? screamed Mr. Peacock.

I am here because of the Dwarf, yelled Mrs. Yellington.

But you were telling me about the chair, cried Mr. Peacock.

The chair is part of it, yelled Mrs. Yellington.

Can you understand the shepherd who has lost a lamb? He cares not for dwarves and giants. Do you think I wish to hear fairy tales? cried Mr. Peacock.

My sister . . . , yelled Mrs. Yellington.

Your sister? screamed Mr. Peacock.

Mrs. Shoutington, shouted Mrs. Yellington.

You and Mrs. Shoutington are sisters? shouted Mr. Peacock.

Of course. . . Never mind the testicles, which are always part of the bargain the woman makes, yelled Mrs. Yellington.

Testicles? screamed Mr. Peacock.

The pourings of which do with the woman so beget . . . , cried Mrs. Yellington.

What talk is that? screamed Mr. Peacock.


**THE BEGOTTEN**

The Dwarf, the Dwarf, son and heir of the elder Peacock, screamed Mr. Yellington.

And the chair? screamed Mr. Peacock.

The chair, it's the Dwarf's, cried Mrs. Yellington.

I see, the Dwarf owns everything, cried Mr. Peacock.

And the Dwarf is mine, yelled Mrs. Yellington.

Are you saying that the Dwarf is the fruit of a union between yourself and my relative? cried Mr. Peacock.

I am saying that he did with me as it is done that the woman so begets, yelled Mrs. Yellington.

And that by the line of the elder Cock, a drop of generative viscosity, I am cheated further from that which is mine, cried Mr. Peacock.

He did with me as it is done the woman that she so begets, yelled Mrs. Yellington.

Are you maneuvering me that I shall do with you as it is done with the woman that she begets, that you shall beget, this time a giant? screamed Mr. Peacock.

No no no, screamed Mrs. Yellington.

I see it now, there is something crooked in the Peacock sperm. And you would use it to populate the world with fairy tale persons; each claiming a share, whittling down my world with freaks, cried Mr. Peacock.

I wish only that you leave my son's home, said Mrs. Yellington.

This is my house. It is my chair that is missing, cried Mr. Peacock.

I'm sure the chair would be turned over to you if you left quietly, said Mrs. Yellington.

The chair without the house is worth as much as the house without the chair, screamed Mr. Peacock.

The chair is easy. But the large debt you've run up . . . , said Mrs. Yellington.

What debt? screamed Mr. Peacock.

Room and board, said Mrs. Yellington.

I don't pay room and board in my own home, screamed Mr. Peacock.

When the Captain of Police beats you with his night stick . . . , said Mrs. Yellington.

Beats me with his nightstick? Perhaps you are unaware that I am under special discipline and care, and that you are not supposed to arouse me sexually. I hope you understand that I have voluntarily committed myself to treatment, said Mr. Peacock.

You shall have a doctor's bill to pay, said Mrs. Yellington.

I am under the care of my servants, who have taken a parental interest in me in view of our age difference. It falls that I, as the junior member of our trinity, am in the relationship of child to the other two, who being senior to the first mentioned member, act the parents in the trinity. I have been put on gruel that I might repent my gluttony; and for which gruel acts the tonic which repairs what was otherwise a most athletic, if not champion, anatomy. Thus, you find me in a state of disrepair. However, I am in repair. And I shall rise again to my excellent conquests on the fields of sport, said Mr. Peacock.

Your words are very touching, sir, sighed Mrs. Yellington.

. . . For having been poorly dealt with by insurgent servants I find it best to give myself over to repair . . . I can feel it happening within me; my moral structures rebuild themselves. Not to mention the toning of muscles grown flabby from worry and depression . . . Not at all helped by the loss of the chair, which has for some time now been a source of deep concern. Perhaps you would be willing to put my mind at rest about the chair? sighed Mr. Peacock.

Of course. It is not my wish to add any further source of disquiet to your over-excited sexual preoccupations, said Mrs. Yellington.

You are very kind, and indeed a woman of the upper-classes, sighed Mr. Peacock.


## THE GOSSIP OF SUMMERS PAST

My sister, Mrs. Shoutington, already well advised as to the wealth of the elder Peacock, set herself the task of winning his favor with a view to marriage. I could not but find his wealth a source of disquiet to my already over-excited sexual preoccupations; which was perhaps more a scientific quest, as to the nature of the male instrumentalities. Which is to say, the pourings of which with the woman so begets . . . , said Mrs. Yellington.

Yes yes, you keep using that phrase, roared Mr. Peacock.

Now the elder Peacock had a maid. And she kept the grocery bills high with large orders of mayonnaise, which she used as a medicine for her rheumatism. This meant frequent applications within viewing distance of the elder Peacock, and a most unsavory caretaker. The application meant the removal of all her clothes, revealing those parts of the woman that men cherish most of all; and are used in the pursuance of wealth, when marriage is the only way. So that both my sister and I were most frustrated by the Maid's free and spontaneous demonstrations of that which we hid to bait the wedding night. My sister said, when in Rome do as the Romans do. So that I immediately set sail for Europe, and lost a summer there. Meanwhile, my sister found a comfortable bed in the elder Peacock's bedroom that summer.

When I returned from Italy I said to my sister, the Romans act just like us. I said, when in Rome do as Mrs. Yellington does; she is quite as Roman as the Romans are . . . , said Mrs. Yellington.

Shut your stupid mouth. Do I wish to hear gossip of summers past. You and your sister make me sick, cried Mr. Peacock.

The fact of the matter is that the Maid has no figure for such exhibitions. While I, with perfect figure, exquisite teats and all, was too much the lady . . . However, the central position was occupied by the elder Peacock's testicles. All else was sheer mimicry of historic attitudes, done to please and woo him to the pourings that so engage the woman in the wifehood . . . , said Mrs. Yellington.

Yes yes yes, and when did the chair begin to figure in these unseemly happenings? screamed Mr. Peacock.

The Maid had begun, as decoy, to lay out her clothes on the chair; perhaps to produce a clothed effigy of herself to better shock with the naked flesh. Where, in the first instance, one took the chair for the Maid; she with little figure, in the sense of its shapelessness. But then, in the second instance, one was aware of a blob of caucasoid pink, glistening like the male member after its pleasure . . . , said Mrs. Yellington.

What are you saying? screamed Mr. Peacock.

Yes, one without further interpretation of fact assumed the chair was the Maid, being so draped as it was. And then the sudden awareness of the female caucasoid blob; spheres imposed upon spheres; the rounded breasts, bearing each a red grape, offering suck . . . , said Mrs. Yellington.

What are you saying? screamed Mr. Peacock.

Yes, the chair, its hind legs wearing the Maid's stockings and underpants; the legs stuck into her shoes, and so forth. Each corresponding part of the chair aptly dressed in relation to the human frame. Was it any wonder that older men with their poor eyes became confused and took the chair, too many times, in the act of the pourings, of which with the woman so begets? yelled Mrs. Yellington.

Are you saying that the chair came to abuse while acting as a wardrobe? cried Mr. Peacock.

I am saying that there was once a chair that lived, even as you and I, which had come to much favor in the master's eye. But alas, the chair fell in with wicked servants, and was lost to the ways of evil, yelled Mrs. Yellington.

Yes yes, screamed Mr. Peacock.

What was at first a life of virtue, turned now toward the shadows of corruption; and so sank down into darkness, yelled Mrs. Yellington.

Stop it, stop it, stop it! I shall choke you to death, screamed Mr. Peacock.

. . . Was it any wonder . . . , said Mrs. Yellington.

I cannot stand your figures of speech, screamed Mr. Peacock.

Oh, I see, you cannot stand my figure. It's only the Maid's you can stand. Frankly, I can see no place here for such an editorial remark. However, there is little doubt in my mind as to who has claim to the best figure, yours notwithstanding, yelled Mrs. Yellington.

# THE BIRD

I have no wish to discuss the physical contours of human beings. I find it all mere hideous necessity. Which for me leaves little room for sensual desire. No more so than the ox at field. And I do hope you will not fall into the asinine trap of sensual descriptions of your physique as regards others. Comparisons only serve to point up the disparity between angel and ape, cried Mr. Peacock.

I cannot allow myself, even by word, to be compromised. I understand that you are working toward a fuller answer to your sexual need. But I assure you, sir, the subtle love-making in your words produces only nausea within me, yelled Mrs. Yellington.

You are quite misunderstanding me. I have no wish to indulge in excretory functions with you. Quite the otherwise. Surely you have not missed seeing this chastity belt when my dress comes up? It is worn not so much that I might abuse the bird of my displeasure, which you see hunched on the eggs that beget in a nest of sexual hair; its one eye closed . . . But that others, seeing this instrumentality of excretory yearnings, might so use me that I would rape them quite beyond my need or pleasure. It is a nervous tic, I believe, as the Maid calls it. And as a further safeguard I wear one of the Maid's old dresses to further discourage the approach of sensualists. So, as you see, I am completely within my discipline. Not that I need the instruction implied by this iron cage, where the bird of my displeasure dwells, until the need to urinate drives it to its next abusive act . . . But that my mind of late has been overweighed with worry concerning the running of the estate; not the least of which is the missing chair, said Mr. Peacock.

I quite understand, sir, and sympathize with you. But I cannot, even in charity, indulge your sexual preoccupations, yelled Mrs. Yellington.

You quite misunderstand, you are far too ugly to arouse any expansion in the bird. Enough of this absurd controversy as to my appetites. You were telling me how the chair came to be missing, screamed Mr. Peacock.

What chair? yelled Mrs. Yellington.

The chair, the chair, screamed Mr. Peacock.

Oh, that chair; the Maid's chair, yelled Mrs. Yellington.

It's not the Maid's chair. It's mine, screamed Mr. Peacock.

I only say, the Maid's chair, to identify it. For in no other way is it marked by any difference, save by the strong smell of the pourings of men, yelled Mrs. Yellington.

Yes yes, of course, the chair through no fault of its own had become involved in several sexual adventures, screamed Mr. Peacock.

. . . A chair living, even as you and I, lost to the ways of evil. What was at first a life of virtue, turned now toward the shadows of corruption . . . , yelled Mrs. Yellington.

And so sank down in darkness! Enough enough, screamed Mr. Peacock.

. . . And so sank down in darkness, yelled Mrs. Yellington.

The chair, the chair, the chair, cried Mr. Peacock.

Well, as I was saying, the root of the trouble, at the high seat of attainment . . . , said Mrs. Yellington.

Enough of those rhetorical involutions, screamed Mr. Peacock.

As I was saying, at the end of the tunnel of struggle, shining like nodules of gold, were the elder Peacock's testes . . . , yelled Mrs. Yellington.

Testes? screamed Mr. Peacock.

The pourings of which with the woman so begets, yelled Mrs. Yellington.

That same phrase. What's wrong with you? Can't you think of anything except the unfortunate excretory functions? cried Mr. Peacock.

You seem to confuse the defecating manifestation with the pourings of milt. Which only proves you to be badly toilet-trained, yelled Mrs. Yellington.

Are you saying that I might wet my bed? screamed Mr. Peacock.

It is not to be discounted, yelled Mrs. Yellington.

I swear I would never do that. Not even if I drank a whole quart of water before retiring, screamed Mr. Peacock.

Which is quite beside the point, yelled Mrs. Yellington.

But you still think I might wet my bed, screamed Mr. Peacock.

I don't care if you shit in your bed. I'm not in the least interested in your excretory functions. Can't you understand that I have come only for justice? yelled Mrs. Yellington.

I am merely trying to make the point that I do not wet the bed, screamed Mr. Peacock.

But if you did wet the bed it could not possibly matter to me, screamed Mrs. Yellington.

What are you saying? screamed Mr. Peacock.

That I am here for justice, not to discuss your medical problems, yelled Mrs. Yellington.

... You had been saying how the chair had become the recipient of unsought-for attentions in the mistaken notion that confused it with the Maid, cried Mr. Peacock.

Precisely. The chair built a reputation for being one of easy virtue. Why then should the elder Peacock court my favor? In fact, my sister, Mrs. Shoutington, lost out because of that wicked chair. Although she gave way to the elder Peacock's pleasure without his having to pay the usual ritual reprisals. Still, the chair asked no such hostage to custom. So that the chair remained in the central position of the elder Peacock's affection. And was able to claim his testicles without contest. It was at this time that my sister took up with the servants. Finding the Caretaker quite unattractive, still, she allowed him certain privilege in lieu of the prime target, that she lose not the rhythm of her readiness. And though the Maid was the source of her trouble, she found it best to tolerate her with a certain sisterliness. And so they passed many an evening together, sipping brandy and exchanging insights, said Mrs. Yellington.

## PEACOCK SLEEPS

Do you mind if I doze as you talk? I feel a little tired, said Mr. Peacock.

Yes yes, the ceilings were all cracked from the incessant rattling of the upstairs activities. The elder Peacock stumbling downstairs at intervals, asking for a sip of brandy, saying with a smirk, what a dame. You might ask where was I. You might well ask. Assuming the question. I was not far, to be sure. I spent many nights on the back porch roof looking into the elder Peacock's window. It was an outrageous scene: The elder Peacock sitting on the chair backwards, his legs around the back of the chair, his arms embracing as his legs, and the whole compaction jumping and skittering along the floor; till it was a wonder that any plaster remained on the ceilings below. Occasionally I would strip in my anguish and display my torso so that he could see it. But alas, he mistook my breasts and pubis for a face. He would shake his fist at me, and then continue in the act that is a pouring, which with the woman so begets. It was a wonder that one so old could achieve that pouring so often. Occasionally driven by high irritation, the Maid would tap on the ceiling with a broom as critical statement to the unending commotion above. Occasionally the servants and my sister would break in on the old man and start beating on his back for surcease from his endless pourings. The room by now had earned an unlovely smell. For he not only poured out his milt, but when that ran dry he would spit, and he would piss and defecate. His room truly became a hell hole of filth. And in the midst of it a white haired, balding old man, his face far too red. His knuckles white with unyielding embrace. His member, never less than at full erection, had become a stony gray. Not to mention his testicle sack, the burden of which in the commotion hung, flung through the spokes of the chair's back, and would not come back through no matter how hard he pulled; which again seemed to stimulate another flowing of that which with the woman so begets. Finally his health was broken. The Caretaker cut the offending spokes to release the old man from his pleasure. They put him to bed. He seemed to have achieved an unending jerking motion and a constant gasping, like a fish removed from the sea. My sister, never giving up, would get into bed with the dying old man, and try to place herself in position that she might receive the pourings, which even now had not ceased. So at times she was successful in achieving what is delicately called, the embrace; for which it must be said the old man was not aware. She sought, as it must be clear, no sensual endowment, but rather the elder Peacock's heir. Now, as I told you, it had become a habit of mine to be outside his window; occasionally displaying myself as attractively as possible. Now I dared to raise the window and enter. Now it was my turn to be with the old man. When the others would enter I would slip under his bed. I would see my sister's ugly feet disappear into his bed. I would hear them, the old Peacock saying, no no, leave it alone; do you take me for an endless fountain? I say let go of pride, and leave the testicles to their own riddle, I've just screwed you! No you didn't, my sister would cry, you're getting so old you don't remember. I remember you, two tits and a hole, what do you take me for, an old man? he would cry. I say stop stroking it, you're going to kill it, and then we'll both be out of luck, he would shout. Finally she would get up and leave. And when he was ready again I would climb back into his bed, smothered in his joy-giving greed . . . Mr. Peacock, are you awake? yelled Mrs. Yellington.

## PEACOCK AWAKENS

Yes, of course, I was just dozing. What are you saying? Did you finally get around to what happened to the chair? cried Mr. Peacock.

The Caretaker removed the chair as an aid toward the old Peacock's healing, yelled Mrs. Yellington.

What? Did he take it? Now we're on to something, screamed Mr. Peacock.

He put it in the kitchen. That's where it belonged anyway. It was one of six kitchen chairs, yelled Mrs. Yellington.

Was this the chair that was finally missing? screamed Mr. Peacock.

That's a question, yelled Mrs. Yellington.

Of course that's a question. We're looking for a chair particularized only in its being lost. Not because it was different before it was lost. Can't you understand what I am after? screamed Mr. Peacock.

The chair, screamed Mrs. Yellington.

Yes. But only because it is missing. If it were not missing I would take no notice of it. There are hundreds of chairs on the estate, do I even notice them? Of course not. But should one begin to be missing, that is quite another thing. It means theft, loss, the draining away of the estate, screamed Mr. Peacock.

Which is not yours anyway, screamed Mrs. Yellington.

What are you saying, you evil woman? screamed Mr. Peacock.

The old Peacock did with me as it is done the woman that she bring forth. Which I did, screamed Mrs. Yellington.

There is a lesson implied in your repetitions about the woman being done to that she brings forth . . . , cried Mr. Peacock.

You are not the rightful heir, you are not the rightful heir, yelled Mrs. Yellington.

Who is, if not I? screamed Mr. Peacock.

He who is closest to the testicles of the elder Peacock, my son, your cousin, the Dwarf, screamed Mrs. Yellington.

What papers prove this pedigree? cried Mr. Peacock.

None, alas, wept Mrs. Yellington.

Then why do you upset me? You are no more than a cat that comes home with kittens. We do not make these kittens, because they happen to be born in the cellar, heirs to the estate. No more than we would make the mice in the walls heirs. Because a petulant and cruel Dwarf claims through his mother, using also wicked servants to insinuate this, that he is master of the Peacock estate, does in no way offer rightful challenge to the Peacock heir, cried Mr. Peacock.

My son has no wish to send you away. He wants you to stay. His only wish is that you occupy one of the rooms set aside for servants. That you, in fact, take on the duties of a servant, yelled Mrs. Yellington.

How may the master do this without actually becoming a servant? screamed Mr. Peacock.

In essence this is what he requires, that you renounce all claim to privilege, and come into the servitude that marks the hired man, yelled Mrs. Yellington.

Be a servant in my own house that I might flatter a dwarf? screamed Mr. Peacock.

That there can only be one master is a source of extreme irritation to my son, in that you make claim to that position, yelled Mrs. Yellington.

I will hear no more of this. Do not let this iron cage of morality enforced deceive you as to the state of my fall, cried Mr. Peacock.

Morality forced speaks to morality abandoned in the first instance, I should think, cried Mrs. Yellington.

The cure speaks only to the symptom, not to the cause, screamed Mr. Peacock.

If the cause be greater than the symptom, then God help you, sir, yelled Mrs. Yellington.

The cause is lost in the metaphysics; and it is there that all men share in my idiopathology, said Mr. Peacock.

Liar liar, you have been found out, and have been restrained from further congenital spread of pollution, screamed Mrs. Yellington.

You will not allow that my torment is a reflection of the immorality of others? cried Mr. Peacock.

## A WOMAN OF THE PEOPLE

The majority speak against you. And until God speaks, who is the best judge of what is good for man, if not man in his greatest number? yelled Mrs. Yellington.

And do you speak for them? cried Mr. Peacock.

They speak for me, and I act with them, yelled Mrs. Yellington.

What is my crime? screamed Mr. Peacock.

You are a criminal, yelled Mrs. Yellington.

Why do you say that? screamed Mr. Peacock.

One feels if one looks away that you are making some furtive movement; that you are touching yourself, or trying to steal something, yelled Mrs. Yellington.

I'm not a stone statue, I have to move. But I can assure you that I do nothing that I shouldn't be proud to demonstrate in front of the highest banking authorities, cried Mr. Peacock.

I don't know, there's something about you; the lack of real purpose. A lack of manhood. One feels that you're a bed-wetter, yelled Mrs. Yellington.

You are confusing nervousness with evil intention, screamed Mr. Peacock.

Am I? How is it you're still in bed? You are hoping that others will bow and scrape to you. You want people to die and leave you things. It is true, that it's impossible to find you in the act of evil. And yet, all about you evil things happen. The old Peacock dies without leaving a proper will. You just happen to be the beneficiary. Your bed is foul with urine. No, nobody sees you pissing. Your bed just happens to be wet. You make furtive movements. No, you're not doing anything; and yet, you're either pulling at yourself, or sneaking something under your dress, screamed Mrs. Yellington.

Get out of my house, screamed Mr. Peacock.

It's my son's house, yelled Mrs. Yellington.

Get out before I have you arrested for violating my peace of mind, screamed Mr. Peacock.

May I remind you that my son has full rights to order the servants about. Whereas you are the titular head of the house, my son, for all practical means is, at least, equally in charge, said Mrs. Yellington.

What does he want, my life? screamed Mr. Peacock.

Merely that you come under his jurisdiction as a servant, which you rightly are, said Mrs. Yellington.

And what advantage do I gain? screamed Mr. Peacock.

The pride in knowing that you did right. And to allow your disciplining, which is well started, as exemplified by the chastity belt you are wearing, to continue; that the servants might minister to your slightest disobedience, said Mrs. Yellington.

Disobedience? Is it possible for me to disobey? I am the one who gives orders. It is the servants who are liable to disobey, screamed Mr. Peacock.

And that is what I am saying, that should you accept servitude you would be in a position to disobey. Then comes the disciplinary part, which would be administered by the servants under the orders of my son, the Dwarf, and rightful heir by his ascendancy from the fluid capacity of the late Peacock, yelled Mrs. Yellington.

Absolutely not. I should prefer to marry the Maid, and thereby secure both house and money, cried Mr. Peacock.

You wouldn't marry your own mother to cheat my son out of his inheritance? yelled Mrs. Yellington.

I know it sounds terrible. But I mean it only as an extreme example of the ends I would go. Surely you cannot think I would marry my own mother? I don't even like girls. Besides which, the Maid is not my mother. Although I do admit the relationship is there. Which is the older female and the younger male. This allows a certain parent and offspring juxtaposition. But one must not conclude that I would not take extreme means to anchor my properties against legal vandalism, cried Mr. Peacock.

## DWARVES

Of course, I quite understand. As my husband, Mr. Yellington, is so often heard to say, a man's home is his castle, said Mrs. Yellington.

Your husband? screamed Mr. Peacock.

Yes, he sometimes helps the Caretaker, said Mrs. Yellington.

You never said you had a husband, cried Mr. Peacock.

What does it matter? He's a dwarf, just like your cousin, said Mrs. Yellington.

Just like your son, screamed Mr. Peacock.

I cannot understand your cruel interest in unfortunate glandular situations. The coincidence of two such unfortunate glandular cases on the estate only compounds the morbidity of your interests, yelled Mrs. Yellington.

Don't you see the connection? screamed Mr. Peacock.

The connection? The coincidence of two such cases; the two most important people in my life. What are you getting at? screamed Mrs. Yellington.

Like father like son, screamed Mr. Peacock.

Are you suggesting that the elder Peacock had sex with my husband, and so produced my son? screamed Mrs. Yellington.

It is rather clear to one of my attainment, that as the birds breed true, so does the Dwarf, said Mr. Peacock.

Are you suggesting that my son and I are the parents of my husband? screamed Mrs. Yellington.

I am suggesting quite the otherwise, said Mr. Peacock.

That my son and my husband are my parents? How can you even dream of such a morbid possibility? screamed Mrs. Yellington.

I am suggesting that you laid with your dwarf husband, and that he did, to use your words, with you that which with the woman so begets; and gave into your womb the dwarf-seed of the dwarf-child, cried Mr. Peacock.

Is that true? screamed Mrs. Yellington.

Notice, and I assure you I know quite a bit about the excretory

functions, that the elder Peacock engaged the excretory attentions of many persons and gave not any of them children, except
you. He gave not child to your sister, Mrs. Shoutington. He gave
not child to the Maid. He gave not child to the Caretaker. And he
gave not child to the chair. Why then does he give you a child?
cried Mr. Peacock.

He liked me best, yelled Mrs. Yellington.

The truth is that the seeds of the old man have not the power to
grow into children. You can grow radishes or spinach with them.
But they cannot make persons, said Mr. Peacock.

It did seem funny to have a dwarf-child and to be married to a
dwarf-husband. It seemed the Lord wanted to surround me with
dwarves. Every place I looked was dwarves, said Mrs. Yellington.

Besides which, the law so states that if a married woman spawn,
such spawn shall be considered the spawn also of the husband,
regardless of the author of said milt, of which the child is the virtue
of, cried Mr. Peacock.

A criminal who is also a lawyer ought to do very well, yelled
Mrs. Yellington.

I think I have disposed of this problem with exceeding deftness.
If only all problems lent themselves to logic, sighed Mr. Peacock.

A criminal who is also a lawyer ought to do very well, screamed
Mrs. Yellington.

Why do you keep saying that? cried Mr. Peacock.

You are a criminal, cried Mrs. Yellington.

Why do you say I am a criminal? screamed Mr. Peacock.

You keep making furtive movements, yelled Mrs. Yellington.

It's not criminal to move, cried Mr. Peacock.

Furtive movements, screamed Mrs. Yellington.

Until proved to the otherwise, you must assume my innocence,
screamed Mr. Peacock.

You're pulling at yourself, or putting things up under your
dress, screamed Mrs. Yellington.

If I'm putting anything up under the my dress I'm putting my
own properties up under my dress. You seem to forget that everything here is mine. I am the inheritor. But I assure you, I am

putting nothing up under my dress. Nor am I pulling at myself. And it distresses me to think you think me capable of sneaking things up under my dress, or idly sensualizing. But more distressing is your brazen commitment to words that do little justice to my position as head of this vast estate. Could you really believe that I would remain in bed all day secreting stolen objects up under my dress, and yet be the master of these large and opulent responsibilities associated with the running of this institution? cried Mr. Peacock.

I nearly caught you! screamed Mrs. Yellington.

At what? screamed Mr. Peacock.

You're doing something funny, yelled Mrs. Yellington.

I swear, I am doing nothing, cried Mr. Peacock.

You're going to get caught one of these times, screamed Mrs. Yellington.

At what? screamed Mr. Peacock.

You're either wetting your bed or stealing something, yelled Mrs. Yellington.

I do not steal, screamed Mr. Peacock.

Didn't you just steal the estate? screamed Mrs. Yellington.

I did not. It's mine. It's mine. It's mine, screamed Mr. Peacock.

I can get no sense out of you. I'll ask my son what is to be done. After all, he is the master here, said Mrs. Yellington.

No no no, screamed Mr. Peacock.

I do wish you would leave matters of decision to those in a position to make decisions. If my son is in command, doesn't that make me second in command? When the matter is settled we'll inform you as to what your duties as servant shall be. Until then you must try to stop putting things up under your dress. It does little to recommend you to household duty. Besides which, though recoverable, the objects you stick up under your dress become contaminated, said Mrs. Yellington.

I shall have you and your dwarves dragged bodily off this estate. And I shall place charges against you and your dwarves for stealing the chair, screamed Mr. Peacock.

Ah, nearly caught you, yelled Mrs. Yellington.

Caught me doing what? screamed Mr. Peacock.

I don't know, but you're doing something funny when my back is turned, yelled Mrs. Yellington.

Get out, get out, screamed Mr. Peacock.

You'll be caught one day, yelled Mrs. Yellington.

Get out before I choke you to death, screamed Mr. Peacock.

You are well on your way to a good hammer blow, screamed Mrs. Yellington.

I'll have no more of that. That was all right in the past. But now that I have taken full command I will not tolerate any such show of disrespect, screamed Mr. Peacock.

I'm going right down and complain to your parents. They'll know how to make you behave . . . What was it? . . . An accumulation of many spankings compounded into the single blow of a hammer . . . They know how to handle you, cried Mrs. Yellington.

I shall specify hammer blows for you, screamed Mr. Peacock.

You shall specify nothing. You shall be in the servants' quarters on call, waiting to carry a tray of slops out of my son's room, cried Mrs. Yellington.

I shall have you hit on the head with a hammer, screamed Mr. Peacock.

Good-bye, yelled Mrs. Yellington.

# The Death of the
# Peacock Dwarf

**M**R. PEACOCK stood in the doorway of the kitchen . . .

Well well, look who's finally decided to come down, said the Maid.

I've just had a terrible interview with a horrible woman named Mrs. Yellington. In future I want all prospective guests screened carefully before they are allowed to take up my valuable time, cried Mr. Peacock.

That was Isidore's mother, said the Maid.

Isidore? screamed Mr. Peacock.

The Dwarf. But he just died, said the Maid.

Died? Oh, that's wonderful news, screamed Mr. Peacock.

I can't see anything wonderful in the death of a dwarf, said the Maid.

No, you can't, because you are necessarily on his side. You servants stick together, even in death, cried Mr. Peacock.

He was like a son to me. So we have decided that you will have to be the new Isidore, said the Maid.

I am Percival Peacock, not Isidore Yellington, screamed Mr. Peacock.

Nevertheless, to continue the illusion you will walk on your knees, said the Maid.

I see. That is to shorten me into a short person, cried Mr. Peacock.

Easily struck when the necessity manifests itself, cried the Maid.

But you never struck the Dwarf. You bowed and scraped before him, cried Mr. Peacock.

But you are not really the Dwarf. Do you think just because we will let you act as a dwarf that you are really the Dwarf? You shall earn a spanking if you take privileges not commensurate to your condition, cried the Maid.

I am far too sensitive to allow myself to be drawn into a point of view that earns contempt. I shall do my best to impersonate without overstepping the bounds of good taste, cried Mr. Peacock.

And you will not use your kneeling position to peer under my dress, cried the Maid.

Your undergarments interest me as much as union suits dancing from a clothes line. In other words, I have not the faintest desire to take advantage of the perspective which belongs to the imitation of the Dwarf, cried Mr. Peacock.

Imitation, only imitation, cried the Maid.

Do you think I wish to do more than imitate? screamed Mr. Peacock.

Who knows what the murderer will do? cried the Maid.

I do not even wish to imitate. I do it only as an act of mercy, screamed Mr. Peacock.

It is the least you can do to fill in for a life you have taken, cried the Maid.

Are you saying I killed the Dwarf? screamed Mr. Peacock.


## THE MARTIAL MATRON

Attention, screamed the Maid.

What do you mean? said Mr. Peacock.

Attention, screamed the Maid.

Why are you being military? screamed Mr. Peacock.

Because you need discipline, cried the Maid.

Why are you disciplining me? cried Mr. Peacock.

Because you are now a soldier in the service of grief, cried the Maid.

I was always a soldier in the service of grief, cried Mr. Peacock.

I said, attention, screamed the Maid.

How dare you speak to your employer in such a manner as to cast doubts on his credibility; using a command word to fix his attention to the service of further commands? cried Mr. Peacock.

I'm sorry, for a moment my rheumatism and your presence acted in adverse mixture to arouse in me a severe military need, cried the Maid.

I shall let it pass this time. But in future I shall take a dim view of such outbursts of military persuasion, cried Mr. Peacock.

Attention, screamed the Maid.

What moves you to repeat that repulsive command, when it serves only to further inflame an already difficult despair? cried Mr. Peacock.

Do you want a slap across the face? cried the Maid.

This is not a military establishment, screamed Mr. Peacock.

Isn't it? said the Maid.

This is a household where servant confronts master in historic combat, based on insinuation and hidden insult. It is not fitting that the servant strike the master. Then the rule is broken, and servant becomes master. This will never do, cried Mr. Peacock.

Attention, screamed the Maid.

Which means I shall stand rigidly awaiting your next command. However, in the master and servant relationship the master is not allowed the luxury of falling under the orders of the servant. No, in his lonely task of leadership, pondering the next lowly task of the servant, who by the laws of decency has fallen under the master's dictates, cried Mr. Peacock.

Oh, so now it becomes the task of the servant to slap the master's face. I am willing if that is the only choice you allow, cried the Maid.

Perhaps you're a man disguised as an old woman for military intelligence? said Mr. Peacock.

I suppose you think that I'm a male homosexual who jumped at the opportunity of dressing in women's clothes, screamed the Maid.

It could be, cried Mr. Peacock.

Look at yourself, wearing an old woman's dress. I wouldn't be a bit surprised to learn that you are a homosexual, cried the Maid.

This dress is worn to tone a sagging moral structure, and has no bearing on sexual intent. Moreover, it represents the strong male debased medicinally, only then to rise, stripped of his chastity belt and dress, freed from the prophylactic, once again the athlete championing honor, cried Mr. Peacock.

Shut up, screamed the Maid.

What do you mean, shut up? Just as I was expressing optimism, just as I was beginning to see the door begin to open . . . Just as it seemed possible again, screamed Mr. Peacock.

Possible? With a figure like yours you are fit only to waddle around the house waiting for customers, cried the Maid.

What customers? Do you mean I shall be a successful man of commerce, an empire builder? cried Mr. Peacock.

I mean dirty men who'll pay for the loan of your cunt, cried the Maid.

Waddling to be sure, only that I have lost some of my structural integrity owing to the loss of muscle tone. Which corresponds in direct proportion to the loss of certain moral structures. Which I

am happy to say move toward repair under the instructive pro-
phylaxis of this dress. Not to mention this cunning device, which
is the cause of much of my waddling, that it restrains the spend-
thrift excretory function, cried Mr. Peacock.

You are talking yourself into a spanking, cried the Maid.

Why, because I show a certain intemperate optimism as regards the return of lost muscle tone? . . . That I impede, in fact, by
rejoicing too early? said Mr. Peacock.

Oh, shut up, screamed the Maid.

Why do you say, shut up, just when I feel my muscle tone re-
turning? cried Mr. Peacock.

If you want a spanking, just continue babbling, screamed the
Maid.

I am naturally cheered by the gradual return of my former good
health, cried Mr. Peacock.

Shut up. I'm trying to think of how to make you into a dwarf,
screamed the Maid.

No no, I'm trying to be my former self. Now you want me to
change into a dwarf. I can't make all these changes. I must think
of my health, screamed Mr. Peacock.

Get down on your knees, screamed the Maid.

No no, I do not want to do sexual crimes, screamed Mr. Peacock.

Get down on your knees, screamed the Maid.

All right, all right, if it acts the prophylactic against some more
dreadful act. I would do something that is the lesser of two evils,
cried Mr. Peacock.

Get down on your knees, screamed the Maid.

All right, all right, but you'll have to hem my dress, said Mr.
Peacock.

I'll hem your mouth if you don't shut up, cried the Maid.

I believe this nonsense has gone far enough. I've tried to coop-
erate owing to your long service with the elder Peacock. I allowed
that an employer might out of charity lend himself to the necessity
of the servant as regards her rituals of grief; keeping all the while
an eye to sanity. In other words, to allow some leeway to an over-

wrought heart which comes at the death of a dwarf without, however, losing my head to the uneducated rhythms of the serving woman, who has neither taste nor proportion in her animal cravings, said Mr. Peacock.

I am touched that you have some humanity, said the Maid.

I am more than angered at your thinking yourself in a position to make such a judgment. And what about my treatments toward the regeneration of my figure and moral standards? cried Mr. Peacock.

I'm afraid it's too late for that, said the Maid.

Too late? Just when I've made my final resolve to enforce all the good things in myself, suddenly it's too late. And I must die without improvement, screamed Mr. Peacock.

Too bad, said the Maid.


## THE LAW OF NATURE

I refuse to die, screamed Mr. Peacock.

I admire your vitality. It speaks well of you. And it is most fitting that one who is still alive still fights to maintain his life. But, whereas I applaud your highly optimistic view of life, still, your life stands in the way of mine. And by the standards you have set for your life, so I set mine. Which concludes your life. It is the law of nature, said the Maid.

I see. If it's the law of nature, one cannot break laws merely to go on living, cried Mr. Peacock.

Your cooperation does you proud, and speaks to the absurdity of such fellows as you, said the Maid.

Thank you so much. I rather felt you were a woman of understanding. Your compliment goes not unheeded by one most grateful to receive it, said Mr. Peacock.

Now shut up, screamed the Maid.

I fail to see how that follows? cried Mr. Peacock.

It's my rheumatism coupled with your presence that sparks to an extreme irritation, cried the Maid.

I quite understand, and applaud your restraint, which under undue load must break now and again, said Mr. Peacock.

Shut up, screamed the Maid.

And again I applaud your restraint. You are a woman, in spite of loathsome appearance, of nobility, said Mr. Peacock.

You sonofabitch, shut up, screamed the Maid.

And again I must applaud you. For I find myself greatly moved by your bravery, which shows in the high restraint you show. I applaud you and wish you every good wish, said Mr. Peacock.

You are truly the son of whom the mother dreams, said the Maid.

You do me too much honor, sighed Mr. Peacock.

Come to me, cried the Maid.

Oh, please, not that, cried Mr. Peacock.

Come to me because I desire you, screamed the Maid.

No no, you quite misunderstand the master and servant relationship, cried Mr. Peacock.

You're going to die anyway, so what does it matter? screamed the Maid.

I say go to your quarters, and wait until you hear the bell of servitude. When it rings move swiftly and quietly through the halls to my presence; whereupon I shall order you to do some humbling thing, cried Mr. Peacock.


**THE EMBRACE**

Kiss my neck, screamed the Maid.

You are old enough to be my mother, screamed Mr. Peacock.

Is the mother not worthy of love? screamed the Maid.

You are not my mother. And I demand that you bend down and kiss my feet as token of your complete submission to my will. Otherwise I shall fire you for insubordination, screamed Mr. Peacock.

I will kiss your feet, screamed the Maid.

Do not kiss my knees, screamed Mr. Peacock.

They are delicious, screamed the Maid.

Do not kiss my thighs, screamed Mr. Peacock.

They are scrumptious loaves, screamed the Maid.

I warn you, the bottom end of my torso is filled with excretions, seeds and filth and unwholesome waters, and loathsome vapors, screamed Mr. Peacock.

Ah, my pleasure, screamed the Maid.

What are you doing? screamed Mr. Peacock.

Unlocking the cage that keeps me from my final pleasure, screamed the Maid.

Your mouth is dangerous. Why do you not talk? Are you nursing a grudge? Some of me is in your mouth, quite by accident, I assure you! . . . I hate to make mention of it, embarrassing as it is, but I believe an excretory protuberance has got caught in your mouth; quite by accident, I assure you. I shall pay all damages! . . . Please, madam, I shall not be able to hold back . . . Madam, you are quite weakening me . . . Your fingers . . . I should think you played the the piano once with quite remarkable results . . . You are embarrassing both of us . . . I hate to make mention of it . . . I simply hate to make mention of it . . . I just simply hate to . . . , cried Mr. Peacock.


## THE PROPOSAL

I want to marry you, screamed the Maid.

No no, when one wets on himself in public he is apt to feel a little awkward . . . , said Mr. Peacock.

Do you love me? cried the Maid.

Love is hardly . . . , said Mr. Peacock.

Do you love me? screamed the Maid.

Love? Love a serving woman? I find the term love extremely unfortunate when used to describe the master and servant relationship, cried Mr. Peacock.

But I cannot marry someone who doesn't love me, screamed the Maid.

I have no intention of marrying you, even though you have viewed me in a most unfortunate circumstance. True, I should marry you out of embarrassment. And it is worth some thought. However, I would be remiss in the general view of what the master and servant relationship is by allowing, as it were, an example to be set by us, simply because an unfortunate accident occurred due to your close proximity to my excretory openings, cried Mr. Peacock.

Are you trying to say you don't love me enough to marry me? screamed the Maid.


## THE CIRCUMSTANCE

I am saying that an unfortunate circumstance has taken place, due, I must say, to your carelessness. Had you kept your mouth closed we might very nicely have passed through this time segment without any unusual occurrence. However, I am placed in the embarrassing position of having wet in front of you; for which I ask your pardon. But had you not been so careless as to have your mouth open, said occurrence might well have been avoided. But owing to a certain proximity, and your mouth being open and, as I have mentioned, a certain proximity, which in itself might have offered no danger. But coupled with your open mouth, the laws of chance, the proximity, the open mouth; not to mention my weak state, which is the primary reason for bed-wetting . . . But in this case, as it has been demonstrated quite to our mutual embarrassment . . . , cried Mr. Peacock.

What are you talking about? screamed the Maid.

The unfortunate circumstance that surrounds our mutual embarrassment, cried Mr. Peacock.

But I would think that my figure would not go unnoticed from now on, cried the Maid.

No more so than the ox in a distant field, cried Mr. Peacock.

And I should think that my figure should become the center of your attention, even for its obvious faults. Which I allow are not more so than many others who have come to high estate with, as I have said, far inferior weaponry, cried the Maid.

What do you take me for, some wretch who cleaves to serving women in dark hallways? Besides which, you are old enough to be my mother. To continue this discussion only perpetuates a situation fraught with difficulties, cried Mr. Peacock.


## DEBT

Get down on your knees, screamed the Maid.

I suppose there's some justice in it? cried Mr. Peacock.

On your knees, screamed the Maid.

I realize I am in your debt . . . Perhaps a small sum of money might cover the injury? Surely, to redo the mischief, though you have every right to demand it, only perpetuates a situation fraught with difficulties. However, if you demand equal payment, I should be less than a gentleman, and all that that implies, if I should refuse. But I beg you not to impose such a sentence, cried Mr. Peacock.

Down on your knees, screamed the Maid.

Then there is no hope for me . . . ? But perhaps I shall erase my first embarrassment, cried Mr. Peacock.

I think we shall have to cut your legs off, cried the Maid.

If you will just lift your skirt the necessity of amputation might be circumvented by an unnatural act. Though scarring to the memory, it leaves the physiology intact. If you can see what I'm trying to say? screamed Mr. Peacock.

Do you think because I am a serving woman that I will lift my skirt for you; particularly with you in such an advantageous position? screamed the Maid.

When the master is asked to get down on his knees it can mean but one thing, that he is being asked to expiate a sin by further sin with a servant, screamed Mr. Peacock.

I am making you into a dwarf, cried the Maid.

But the servant is on thin ice if she expects her master to do anything but an unnatural act in payment of the debt so owed the servant. Other than that, all requests, no matter how flattering, are mere insubordinations, which then puts the servant in the master's debt, cried Mr. Peacock.

What is all this banking business? screamed the Maid.

To describe in circumvention what one scarce allows the tongue to describe more directly, cried Mr. Peacock.

Which is what? screamed the Maid.

That which I estimate to be more wicked in words than in the act, cried Mr. Peacock.

. . . I lift my skirt waiving my embarrassment to your pleasure. Does it gain me the stick to beat you into submission? screamed the Maid.

No. It frees me to order you from the room, screamed Mr. Peacock.

You do not pay in kind, sir, screamed the Maid.

If you will let me expiate in like manner as was done you by a proximity not quite fully understood . . . The protuberance of the excretory instrumentality, and the proximity of the oral receptive capacity . . . To put it as delicately as taste and manners prescribe. . . . To expiate in like manner, with a view toward freedom from sin . . . Two sins acting to create one virtue, as it were, semantically. . . That each sin erases the other, and in the absence of sin virtue is found, said Mr. Peacock.

And then shall I order you from the room? screamed the Maid.

No, for then the proximity shall have been reversed, and the former condition shall obtain, where the master orders the servant from the room with abrupt dismissal; perhaps with a kick in the ass to aid the servant's flight. Or would that seem, after a moment's reflection, an unseemly lowering of standards? cried Mr. Peacock.

I think the kick in the ass would be best administered by the servant as she orders a worthless fellow into quietude as her whim requires, cried the Maid.

After the expiation of sin the master looks at the servant rather oddly, not quite believing that she would lift her foot against him. But after a few moments he realizes that this is exactly what she did. But, due to his delicate upbringing, he is rather taxed as to what to do in answer to this unprovoked break in discipline, cried Mr. Peacock.

And so she kicks his highness again so that the point of her shoe is driven into his asshole, screamed the Maid.

This triggers a series of responses; that an excretory instrumentality should have its repose disturbed by an unnatural entry; the embarrassment that such an entry admits to the existence of such an instrumentality; that now the master withholds no secret from the servant. Speculation as to the deity of the master is put aside, and replaced by contempt of the servant for the master, screamed Mr. Peacock.

So is the master paid for asking the serving woman to lift her skirt, cried the Maid.

# Peacock the Seducer

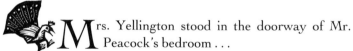rs. Yellington stood in the doorway of Mr. Peacock's bedroom . . .

What are you doing in my room? cried Mr. Peacock.

Isidore is dead, said Mrs. Yellington.

But the living must sleep, cried Mr. Peacock.

But I'm not tired, said Mrs. Yellington.

I was speaking of myself. Having put a full day in, I assure I have earned a fatigue paid only by a night of sleep, cried Mr. Peacock.

But you will wake up tomorrow, and Isidore will still be dead, said Mrs. Yellington.

And he will be dead every day that I wake up, until I am dead.

Are you trying to put his death above mine? screamed Mr. Peacock.

But you are a servant. When you die we just interview applicants and choose one to fill your position, said Mrs. Yellington.

Quite the contrary, madam. What we do is to interview some dwarves, and choose one to fill your son's position. I quite realize that grief is a distorting lens. But, if you will look more carefully, you will see a master of a vast estate, who might have just returned from the hunt, or from chastising some wicked servant . . . He moves with a presence that is unmistakable . . . , said Mr. Peacock.

I see a wicked servant. He is wearing an old woman's dress for the purpose of inviting the courtship of other men, said Mrs. Yellington.

No no, you must look past this old dress and see a great hunting coat of rough fur . . . See how I walk, the authority there . . . The manly weight of muscles . . . , said Mr. Peacock.

Oh, please, you are too terrible. And what are you doing in the family rooms? You're supposed to be in the servants' quarters listening for the bell that rings you to service. I'm expecting Mrs. Shoutington. You may prepare a service for four; brandy and sweetmeats, said Mrs. Yellington.

Four? cried Mr. Peacock.

Myself, my sister, Mrs. Shoutington, the Maid and the Caretaker. How dare you question me? cried Mrs. Yellington.

I allow that grief acts the distorting lens . . . , said Mr. Peacock.

Get to the servants' quarters immediately, screamed Mrs. Yellington.

I believe you have not fully grasped the situation. What you view is an athlete, as well as a master of a vast estate. He steps boldly into his bedroom with a certain style that is unmistakably the mark of his high birth. He wears with eccentric assertion a rough hunting coat; mingled in the fur are twigs and moss. He dominates the room. All shrink under the weight of his presence. . . , said Mr. Peacock.

I said go to the servants' quarters. They'll supply you with the proper dress and apron, shouted Mrs. Yellington.

No, I am to be seen in a white dinner jacket; a red carnation in the button hole. The ladies are most enchanted with this man of mysteries. The white dinner jacket cannot hide the gorilla musculature beneath. A woman across the room asks, who is that charming man? A small applause breaks out. People are suddenly and spontaneously given to applauding the image I present. Suddenly they are cheering. I try not to notice, presenting a humble superiority that acts the filter, which wards off the hatred of envy, to light my pride, said Mr. Peacock.

If you do not return to your proper duties at once I shall have no option, but to call the Captain of Police, cried Mrs. Yellington.

I have allowed that grief acts the distorting lens . . . And, in lieu of sense, I have put gentleness to gain you time to recompose your virtue. However, gentleness eats out the patience. I am out of patience with you. And in the place of the wasted patience is anger. Beware the deferred anger! screamed Mr. Peacock.

I don't want to fight with you, you are an old woman. There's no contest there. I should call the Captain of Police and ask him to bring a prison matron along to handle you. However, it looks bad that the mistress needs to call in an outside authority to handle her servants. I ask you again to comply to the rules of servitude and retire to the servants' quarters, yelled Mrs. Yellington.

Get out of here, screamed Mr. Peacock.

I shall call the others. Others. Others! screamed Mrs. Yellington.

I shall choke you to death, cried Mr. Peacock.

Others. Others! screamed Mrs. Yellington.

What is it? cried a voice from below.

The serving woman refuses to be ordered about. Come quickly, screamed Mrs. Yellington.

Should the Caretaker bring his hammer? cried a voice from below.

Others, others, come quickly, screamed Mrs. Yellington.

No no, the brandy is so good that we waive our punitive rights against the mutinous serving woman, cried a voice from below.

The ship of authority is sinking, screamed Mrs. Yellington.

Now Mr. Peacock moves, taking advantage in that classical proportion; in that there is a falling out between wicked servants, a disparity of aims; and in that fracturing Mr. Peacock seizes one rein and then another, cried Mr. Peacock.

Do not come near me, screamed Mrs. Yellington.

Discipline now takes a physical bent. Master and servant come to contest. Heaven holds its breath, cried Mr. Peacock.

I should be perfectly willing to retreat without injury, screamed Mrs. Yellington.

It is too late. Authority wounded is authority aroused. Authority aroused is authority punitive, cried Mr. Peacock.

No no, I will allow that I am a serving woman, screamed Mrs. Yellington.

Then go to the servants' quarters, and remain there until you hear me yawn. Let that act as the signal for you to prepare my breakfast, said Mr. Peacock.


## BUT IT IS TOO LATE

Oh, no, it is too late. Now we must get married, cried Mrs. Yellington.

Marry a serving woman? screamed Mr. Peacock.

Yes, I have been compromised by you, cried Mrs. Yellington.

I have done nothing, screamed Mr. Peacock.

The proximity speaks to the difficulty, cried Mrs. Yellington.

I will have none of it. I cannot marry serving people. No no, it is quite impossible, screamed Mr. Peacock.

If I bear your child . . . , said Mrs. Yellington.

Don't you dare, screamed Mr. Peacock.

It is too late, said Mrs. Yellington.

I did not that which is done which puffs the woman into the maternal nuisance. Nor have I even blown a kiss in your direction, screamed Mr. Peacock.

It is the proximity that speaks to the difficulty, said Mrs. Yellington.

Not one dirty thought, screamed Mr. Peacock.

Star-crossed lovers, screamed Mrs. Yellington.

Pawns in the class struggle . . . Romantic nonsense . . . Fabrication . . . Reductio ad absurdum, screamed Mr. Peacock.

Others, others, screamed Mrs. Yellington.

Why are you calling the others? cried Mr. Peacock.

I shall have to ask their permission, said Mrs. Yellington.

You shall ask my permission. Which I withhold on the grounds that I have had not one dirty thought, screamed Mr. Peacock.

Do you love me? cried Mrs. Yellington.

No no, not one dirty thought, screamed Mr. Peacock.

A marriage of convenience, as they say, cried Mrs. Yellington.

No no, it is not convenient, cried Mr. Peacock.

My husband will be the best man, cried Mrs. Yellington.

No no, twin husbands tend toward dissatisfaction. A rivalry sublimated to sibling demands, and the wife becomes mother to two male children reduced to pre-pubescence. Then in steps the law, which must spank the children that they come to the yoke of manhood without whimper. No no, it is illegal for two husbands to be yoked to one cart . . . Whereas a team, indeed, it does violence to the law. It causes breast-beating among the police; till tired of self-abuse they must turn their nightsticks from symptom to cause, cried Mr. Peacock.

If you invite a woman to your bedroom you must marry her, cried Mrs. Yellington.

But, my scarlet woman, I did not invite you here. You came to gain my servitude, thinking that I was a serving woman, cried Mr. Peacock.

Then the choice is yours. Either you are a seducer or a serving woman, said Mrs. Yellington.

There is always death, said Mr. Peacock.

The dead serving woman, the dead seducer, cried Mrs. Yellington.

In life it is better to be a serving woman than a seducer. Then none may say he had any thoughts other than the conventional prescriptions for dirty dishes. Which, though without applause, is still within virtue, cried Mr. Peacock.

Then why do you bleat at me like an old female sheep, deciding whether to be shorn or whether to be shorn? When the course is obvious, take it. You weary creation, yelled Mrs. Yellington.

## OF THE THRONE

At the root is theft, screamed Mr. Peacock.

To servitude, yelled Mrs. Yellington.

If the chair . . . , cried Mr. Peacock.

What of that? yelled Mrs. Yellington.

In the chair was authority, cried Mr. Peacock.

The sensual decoy, yelled Mrs. Yellington.

The chair debased by the rheumatoid Maid, cried Mr. Peacock.

Taken for the womanhood, yelled Mrs. Yellington.

And so it follows . . . , said Mr. Peacock.

What? screamed Mrs. Yellington.

That from first theft the ray of loss widens in progressing contagion; till wit and flesh, both sagging, speak to the remedial sanctions. And gruel becomes the food of flesh, and indignity comes to discipline the mind . . . The kingdom lost in the loss of a throne . . . Kings knew the power of the chair. There they sat blowing secret farts into the cushioned golden mount . . . , said Mr. Peacock.

To servitude, screamed Mrs. Yellington.

. . . And it was the chair that gave power. That he who sat so, in that repose, was king. It is the chair which gives power. Else than that are the restless of servitude, and need that task which gives reason to momentum, said Mr. Peacock.

The chair, the chair, the chair, yelled Mrs. Yellington.

At the root of authority, cried Mr. Peacock.

Don't you remember? cried Mrs. Yellington.

I try, I try, cried Mr. Peacock.

That which is put by for the further reaching, said Mrs. Yellington.

Yes yes, I reach for your meaning, screamed Mr. Peacock.

The instrument of the first instruction, said Mrs. Yellington.

The rage that defends survival? cried Mr. Peacock.

The first instrumentality of the sitting function, said Mrs. Yellington.

Which is that he sits that he may so profit, screamed Mr. Peacock.

That he earns no punitive reprisal, said Mrs. Yellington.

And so he sits and gains ascendancy, screamed Mr. Peacock.

Over his stool, yelled Mrs. Yellington.

He that sits on a stool dominates said stool, cried Mr. Peacock.

He is befouled, and so gains punitive instruction, screamed Mrs. Yellington.

How dare anyone strike the king? cried Mr. Peacock.

For he is befouled in his own waste. And the matron despairs, and again shoots out the digital organ into the face of the offending factor, the child of her dissatisfaction, cried Mrs. Yellington.

What are you saying? screamed Mr. Peacock.

The child that beshits itself, in spite of all encouragement and threat, removes itself from the maternal patience, and must suffer the maternal rage, said Mrs. Yellington.

But why are you talking about excrement? roared Mr. Peacock.

For therein is the root, cried Mrs. Yellington.

. . . Of putrefaction and all that inhibits the song; the rectumless flight of angels . . . , sighed Mr. Peacock.

Potty-chair, potty-chair, screamed Mrs. Yellington.

The chair that is missing? screamed Mr. Peacock.

The chink in the armor of your wits, cried Mrs. Yellington.

First instrumentality of the sitting? screamed Mr. Peacock.

Does the serving woman understand? screamed Mrs. Yellington.

The chair? screamed Mr. Peacock.

To servitude, yelled Mrs. Yellington.

A dwarf-chair with a hole in the seat? cried Mr. Peacock.

Isidore was my son, wept Mrs. Yellington.

If a dwarf-chair was my childhood chair, was Isidore Yellington my childhood self? cried Mr. Peacock.

Oh, you are too cruel, wept Mrs. Yellington.

Was the chair truly his chair? screamed Mr. Peacock.

Potty-chair, potty-chair, roared Mrs. Yellington.

Is that how the throne is lost to the child? cried Mr. Peacock.

You can have your old chair. It is foul with childish shit, yelled Mrs. Yellington.

Nothing real, only symbols, screamed Mr. Peacock.

If poor Isidore used it, what harm in that? screamed Mrs. Yellington.

Are you saying that the chair is a potty-chair? screamed Mr. Peacock.

You shall earn a spanking, that's for sure, yelled Mrs. Yellington.

No no, it is that I am close to the secret of my longing, howled Mr. Peacock.

Because poor Isidore used the chair, was that wrong? wept Mrs. Yellington.

Not if it be that the Dwarf is the child of me, said Mr. Peacock.

He was the master of this house, screamed Mrs. Yellington.

It is all symbol, screamed Mr. Peacock.

He was a man and you are a woman. He was the master and you are a servant, yelled Mrs. Yellington.

He and I were both master in the mystically stuffed image, said Mr. Peacock.

No no, you are a serving woman, cried Mrs. Yellington.

No no, I take nothing from him, cried Mr. Peacock.

How dare you take something from Isidore? screamed Mrs. Yellington.

No no, I enhance by depth, with orchestration, cried Mr. Peacock.

Don't you dare play the funeral march, screamed Mrs. Yellington.

Can't you see the double image, child and man, serving woman and master? Now merging in mystical oneness! screamed Mr. Peacock.

Clean the house, roared Mrs. Yellington.

You are missing the meaning, cried Mr. Peacock.

You shall be handcuffed to a slops rag, screamed Mrs. Yellington.

I am not a serving lady, cried Mr. Peacock.

Seducer, screamed Mrs. Yellington.

You are quite missing the point, screamed Mr. Peacock.

You shall be handcuffed to a toilet tissue, screamed Mrs. Yellington.

No no, the master is never handcuffed, he is too busy deciding who else is to be handcuffed. It does not do for the master to go about handcuffed. For too many times he needs to use his hand to slap a servant by way of instruction, cried Mr. Peacock.

You shall be handcuffed to dwarves' underwear, screamed Mrs. Yellington.

I think you are quite missing the point, said Mr. Peacock.

Seducer, screamed Mrs. Yellington.

Get out, get out, roared Mr. Peacock.

Too late, we shall have to get married, cried Mrs. Yellington.

It is never too late, screamed Mr. Peacock.

Too late, yelled Mrs. Yellington.

Get out, get out, screamed Mr. Peacock.

Very well, but I shall have a baby tonight; you'll see, yelled Mrs. Yellington.

Not one dirty thought, cried Mr. Peacock.

Compromised, yelled Mrs. Yellington.

Get out, get out, screamed Mr. Peacock.

I'm going to my room and have a baby, yelled Mrs. Yellington.

Don't you dare. Control yourself. Use the bathroom. How dare you have a baby in my house? I shall call the fire department, roared Mr. Peacock.

Baby baby, screamed Mrs. Yellington.

# Peacock Accused

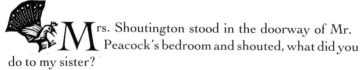Mrs. Shoutington stood in the doorway of Mr.
Peacock's bedroom and shouted, what did you
do to my sister?

I didn't do anything to anybody's sister. I am asleep, sighed Mr.
Peacock.

She had a baby last night, shouted Mrs. Shoutington.

How dare you announce the calving of a servant so early in the
morning. That the estate is richer in beasts is a source of economic
pleasure, to be sure, but hardly to be heralded to the master re-
storing himself in sleep. Tell the herdsman and the butcher, and
give the bull an extra portion of whatever feeds his pleasure, cried
Mr. Peacock.

You cannot blame the bull, screamed Mrs. Shoutington.

No blame to him. He is to be commended for looking to the economic refreshment of the estate. Who blames the bull? cried Mr. Peacock.

But the bull is not Mr. Peacock, screamed Mrs. Shoutington.

What foolishness is that? A bull dare not rise out of the pasture and claim my inheritance. I will have none of it, screamed Mr. Peacock.

You are the father, roared Mrs. Shoutington.

I am not the father of a bull, screamed Mr. Peacock.

You are the father of Mrs. Yellington's baby, cried Mrs. Shoutington.

A tragic proximity . . . I shall pay all damages, screamed Mr. Peacock.

You will marry her, said Mrs. Shoutington.

No no, I shall pay all damages caused by the bull. Certainly a legal responsibility. I should be less than responsible were I to leave the matter where it now hangs. Precariously, as it were, over a moral abyss, cried Mr. Peacock.

Then you will do the right thing? said Mrs. Shoutington.

I said I will pay all damages. If you will see my lawyer he will see to the paying for the damage to your fence or shrubs, or whatever it was that the bull trampled. Now will you please leave? said Mr. Peacock.

You are the father of my sister's child, screamed Mrs. Shoutington.

Out! Out! Do you think I would lay with the bull's mate? Do you think that I have fallen so low that I would cuckold a bull? How dare you accuse me of entertaining an eroticism for a cow? screamed Mr. Peacock.

I am not talking about a cow, cried Mrs. Shoutington.

Then why are you bothering me about a cow? screamed Mr. Peacock.

It is my sister, screamed Mrs. Shoutington.

Then you are a cow, too. What right have you to wander through the house? You might very well befoul the rugs. How dare you befoul the rugs? screamed Mr. Peacock.

No no no! My sister is a human being, cried Mrs. Shoutington.

Oh, I see, your sister is a cow disguised as a human being to gain access to the pleasures of my house, cried Mr. Peacock.

No no, you had sexual intercourse with my sister, who is the mistress of this house. And though you are but a lowly servant, there remains only one moral option, that you and your mistress marry, shouted Mrs. Shoutington.

No no, it is too terrible, all these implications . . . I would prefer to sleep . . . No no, it is best that I continue to sleep, said Mr. Peacock.

# Peacock Prepares
# for Marriage

The Caretaker stood in the doorway of Mr. Peacock's bedroom and whimpered, oh, Mr. Wedlock.

What is it? moaned Mr. Peacock.

It's getting late, whimpered the Caretaker.

Late? screamed Mr. Peacock.

The Captain of Police is down below waiting to marry us, said the Caretaker.

Why are you dressed in a woman's white gown? cried Mr. Peacock.

This is my wedding dress, said the Caretaker.

Wedding dress? screamed Mr. Peacock.

You're going to be my bride, said the Caretaker.

I would rather marry a cow, roared Mr. Peacock.

All the cows are in the north pasture, sir, said the Caretaker.

I thought I was supposed to marry Mrs. Yellington? cried Mr. Peacock.

I'm taking her place, said the Caretaker.

I'm not marrying an old man in a wedding gown, screamed Mr. Peacock.

But I'm your father, that makes all the difference, said the Caretaker.

No no, those flowers in your hair look ugly, screamed Mr. Peacock.

You're not to say things like that to your bride, whimpered the Caretaker.


The Maid stood in the doorway of Mr. Peacock's bedroom and said, hurry up.

I think he's wet his bed, said the Caretaker.

Never mind. Put this wedding gown on Mr. Peacock, said the Maid.

But he's wearing one, cried Mr. Peacock.

Yours is every bit as pretty, said the Maid.

Two men disguised as women can't get married. It looks funny for two brides to be getting married. No, I will have none of it, screamed Mr. Peacock.

Two brides; it's the most natural thing. Do you mean to say you would rather wear a street dress than your pretty wedding gown? said the Maid.

Two women in white being joined in holy matrimony, screamed Mr. Peacock.

Oh, stop your screaming. Of course you're upset. But to vent your confusion by screaming is most unladylike, said the Maid.

The athlete does not wear a wedding gown, screamed Mr. Peacock.

Please be nice, we don't want to upset the Captain of Police, said the Caretaker.

Doesn't the Caretaker look stunning? said the Maid.

He looks hideous; an old man in a wedding gown. I can see his overalls under his gown; and those work shoes. Do you really think I would choose to marry a bride wearing work shoes? And besides, he hasn't shaved for a week, screamed Mr. Peacock.

Did I say my figure is better than yours? whimpered the Caretaker.

Are you comparing your bent old man's figure with the master's? screamed Mr. Peacock.

Oh, stop it, both of you. If comparisons are apt at a time like this, then surely my figure ought to come to prominence for its outstanding conformation to the ideals of womanhood, said the Maid.

As much so as an ox browsing in a distant field, cried Mr. Peacock.

Never mind, just slip into your wedding gown, said the Maid.

This old woman's dress that I am wearing is quite contrary to the spirit of my youth. And, whereas from a strictly gender point of view, this wedding gown does nothing to further the image of manhood. Still, it is closer to the spirit of my youthful purity, cried Mr. Peacock.

Would you like the Captain of Police to spank your head with his nightstick? cried the Maid.

What are you saying? screamed Mr. Peacock.

He's downstairs waiting to marry you and the Caretaker, and you're making him very impatient, said the Maid.

Isn't that too bad, a servant grows impatient; the master had best beware. Are you joking? screamed Mr. Peacock.

Just get into your wedding gown, cried the Maid.

. . . It's a perfect fit. Which speaks to the perfection of my figure no matter in what gender it is presented, said Mr. Peacock.

Oh, you have a lovely figure, said the Caretaker.

Keep your hands off my wedding gown, screamed Mr. Peacock.

I was just straightening it, whimpered the Caretaker.

I said take your hands off my sitting organ, screamed Mr. Peacock.

Your gown was stuck between your cheeks, sir, whimpered the Caretaker.

Are you daring to discuss an area reserved to idealism? screamed Mr. Peacock.

No, I was just pulling your dress out from where it was caught, whimpered the Caretaker.

You will leave such matters of personal decoration to me, screamed Mr. Peacock.

Shut up, both of you. If you can't keep your hands off the Caretaker I'll have to call the Captain of Police, cried the Maid.

He's touching my lower back in such manner that I can only conclude that his hands are sensually motivated. And I felt that I should speak at this time to cancel further encroachments on good taste, said Mr. Peacock.

Never mind. Here, help me into my gown, cried the Maid.

You're not wearing a wedding dress, too? screamed Mr. Peacock.

And why not, am I not going to the wedding? cried the Maid.

Yes, but . . . , said Mr. Peacock.

But nothing. Here, zip me up; and keep your hands to yourself, said the Maid.

If you are suggesting that I would take the opportunity of zipping up your dress to gain sensual access to your person, you have quite misjudged my virtue, cried Mr. Peacock.

Who has to get married? screamed the Maid.

Are you insinuating that I have dirty thoughts? screamed Mr. Peacock.

Who gave who a baby, you seducer? cried the Maid.

That's a lie. I don't even own a baby, screamed Mr. Peacock.

You seduced Mrs. Yellington, and now you are forced to marry her, cried the Maid.

Then why is the Caretaker dressed in a wedding gown? screamed Mr. Peacock.

Because he's your bride, cried the Maid.

But I didn't give him a baby, screamed Mr. Peacock.

What of that? screamed the Maid.

If I have to marry, why am I not marrying Mrs. Yellington? cried Mr. Peacock.

Because she's already married to Mr. Yellington. And why are you asking foolish questions? cried the Maid.

But if she's already married the difficulty is solved, cried Mr. Peacock.

If a man gives a woman a child, no matter what happens, he must get married. It's the law, screamed the Maid.

No no, I will not marry an old man, screamed Mr. Peacock.

It's the law; for which instruction is easily given by the Captain of Police through the office of his nightstick, cried the Maid.

Why are you crying, Mr. Old Man Caretaker? screamed Mr. Peacock.

Because I'm going to have a baby, and it makes me belch, whimpered the Caretaker.

A baby doesn't make you belch, screamed Mr. Peacock.

Yes it does, roared the Maid.

Besides, only women have babies, cried Mr. Peacock.

You're very crude, said the Maid.

No no, it's biological, cried Mr. Peacock.

You have always to lead the conversation into sensually oriented areas. It's a form of perversion, cried the Maid.

No no, I quite assure you that the instrumentalities associated with the matters you refer to ... No no, I quite assure you ... And I shall pay all damages ... If you will please see my lawyer ..., said Mr. Peacock.

Lawyer? Are you trying to divorce me, Mr. Wedlock? whimpered the Caretaker.

I am only marrying you to expiate a debt incurred by a difficult proximity. But in name only. More than that would involve certain lapses into poor taste, screamed Mr. Peacock.

Ladies ladies, I must ask you to lower your voices, cried the Maid.

But I shall do no more than take on a titular partnership in this nuptial recourse, cried Mr. Peacock.

Let us descend, said the Maid.

Indeed, cried Mr. Peacock.

Hold my train, Mr. Wedlock, sighed the Caretaker.

You will hold my train, because you are a servant, cried Mr. Peacock.

Ladies, hold your own trains, cried the Maid.

# Peacock's Wedding

They stood in the doorway of ceremony . . .
Why is the Captain of Police wearing a wedding
gown? screamed, Mr. Peacock.

I have a perfect right to look as nice as everyone else, said the
Captain.

But Mrs. Shoutington and Mrs. Yellington are wearing wedding gowns, too, screamed Mr. Peacock.

Hush up, they have as much right as you to look their best. I
can't understand why you are so selfish? cried the Maid.

It's hideous, screamed Mr. Peacock.

If you don't behave you'll be sent to your room, said the Maid.

But I'm the one getting married, cried Mr. Peacock.

But if you don't behave you will be sent to your room, and somebody else will marry the Caretaker, cried the Maid.

I'm only going through with this to expiate a debt incurred . . . It was by sheer accident, to be laid at the door of nature, which men take upon themselves in the illusion that they have some control. So that I bow to human logic, faulty as it is, and lay waste my claim to innocence. And by so doing expiate in the manner prescribed in the book of etiquette, said Mr. Peacock.

If you refuse to settle down you'll be sent to your room. Surely you must be aware that this is a solemn occasion? said the Maid.

I am quite appraised of the matter at hand, madam, and work only toward its fulfillment, easing the way with words; giving sanction and sense to a ritual rooted past memory in the dark earth of barbaric need . . . To, as it were, give the fluid of words as oil to abbreviate the friction of the mechanical ritual, said Mr. Peacock.

This is not the time for hysterics, cried the Maid.

But quite the contrary, Madam serving woman, I am in full control of myself. No less so than the splendid athlete on the field of honor. I wish only, as I have said, to give easy avenue to cere-monial justice, to bring to fulfillment a judgment equitable to both man and nature. But, by no means to bring impediment to this vehicle of our attention. No, quite the otherwise; rather that I might prepare the road, as it were, to smooth the way, that those at the heart of this meeting might rise to true virtuosity. To say that I would aid those forces that end the orderly procession is rather to say that I am not Mr. Peacock. But once admitting that I am Mr. Peacock, all doubt regarding my propensity for valor, as against the vile and sordid, must lose meaning, if words have value, said Mr. Peacock.

Do you want to be sent to your room this very minute? screamed the Maid.

I believe the good Captain of Police will appreciate the fine sentiment of my words, and see that in no way have I run cross-grain to the august mood. No, rather that I build toward it more fully in a narrative tutored by the gentle acquiescence of tongue to sense, said Mr. Peacock.

Are you going to behave? said the Captain of Police.

Behave? That is a word usually applied to a child, screamed Mr. Peacock.

Does the authority have a right to hit the bride on the head with a nightstick? cried the Captain.

I think not, sir, that is a violation to the dignity and ceremonial integrity of the bride, cried Mr. Peacock.

Well, then behave, screamed the Captain.


## THE CHILD OF THE SEDUCTION

Indeed, Mr. Badcock, haven't you done enough damage already? Look at poor Mrs. Yellington with her new baby. All on account of you, said the Maid.

What is that thing she is holding? cried Mr. Peacock.

The child of your seduction, said the Maid.

That's a pig. She's holding a pig! screamed Mr. Peacock.

What's the difference? cried the Maid.

It's wearing a wedding gown, just like mine. A baby pig is wearing a wedding gown just like mine, screamed Mr. Peacock.

No one said it wasn't a pig. One can love a pig as well as a child. There is no reason to say that because it is a pig that it is unworthy of love, said the Maid.

I thought she had a baby, screamed Mr. Peacock.

Well, if she didn't, she went down to the pigpen and got a pig. Pigs are not beyond love, cried the Maid.

I think you are being very improperly cruel in your personal remarks, shouted Mrs. Shoutington.

I did not mean to suggest that the pig is not due all human privilege . . . Indeed, I would fight to my very last breath to insure equal justice to both pig and man. However, it must not be inferred that I am the father of the specimen in question, however flattering that might be. But you will see that some doubt is cast on the need for the wedding ceremonial. If I may be so bold as to bring up a legal point? said Mr. Peacock.

Is it your desire to embarrass your bride? said the Maid.

I would rather die than bring the rose of shame to my bride's cheek. But the Caretaker will surely renounce his privilege when he sees that the expiation is taken without sin; and he shall have lost no modesty owed the maiden, said Mr. Peacock.

Go to your room this minute, cried the Maid.


## MR. PEACOCK'S FATE

I do not hold that the pig is not to be loved. Here, I will kiss it as proof that I do not think the pig is outside the human concern. If I have offended by word or deed I shall pay all damages. You have only to see my lawyer. The cashier will pay you on the way out. Here, my personal check. If further proof is needed, I would most certainly be willing to marry the pig, and spend the rest of my days in repentant devotion, cried Mr. Peacock.

The pig is not sure, said the Maid.

Of what? screamed Mr. Peacock.

Whether it would be willing to take you on as its bride, said the Maid.

. . . Take me on as its bride, its sow? That I might bulge with piglets. Lying in the pigpen as they suck my pig tits! What sort of life is that for a man of action? screamed Mr. Peacock.

The pig isn't sure, said the Maid.

Does it doubt my worth? How dare an animal contemplate the worth of a human being; pondering his suitability to suckle its young? screamed Mr. Peacock.

Very well, the pig is thinking, said the Maid.

What does the pig decide for the master? screamed Mr. Peacock.

It is not sure that the material possession is everything . . . Could a pig find happiness as the master of a great house? It is a question not lightly decided, said the Maid.

Oh no, that is out of the question. By night its bride, perhaps?

But by day, Mr. Peacock, hunter and athlete, man about town . . . , cried Mr. Peacock.

May I sing? Is it time for song? yelled Mrs. Yellington.

At a time like this, when Mr. Pighock's fate hangs on the whim of a pig, is certainly not the time for joyous song, said the Maid.

I want to sing of a chair that lived, even as you and I, which had come to much favor in its master's eye . . . , yelled Mrs. Yellington.

No no, my nightstick hungers, cried the Captain.

What satisfies its sweet tooth? cried the Maid.

The confection of the blow upon a head, cried the Captain.

Punitive candy, screamed the Maid.

. . . And the testicle song, the pourings of which . . . , screamed Mrs. Yellington.

The marriage goes poorly. But what did one expect in giving matters of grave moral implication into the hands of servants? said Mr. Peacock.


## FIGURES

But have you noticed, Mr. Naughtycock, the opportunity presented? Which is to say, that since we are all wearing wedding gowns, a comparison of figures, a categorizing of physiological contour . . . , said Mrs. Shoutington.

An opportunity for what? To judge the figures of servants? screamed Mr. Peacock.

To give proper due to a figure shouting for proper acclaim, shouted Mrs. Shoutington.

Shrivelly hips, cried the Maid.

Why, you're built like an ox. Mr. Petcock said you are of no more interest than an ox, screamed Mrs. Shoutington.

My dear sirs, I believe that this wedding gown that I am wearing rather accents a superb military bearing; and points to an official type, who stands for no nonsense, said the Captain.

My pig, my pig, yelled Mrs. Yellington.

An excellent example of swine, to be sure. Not lessened to any degree for having been offered up to Mr. Swinecock's embrace. However, by fair appraisal, my figure should bear far to the fore. Leaving in the dust those of lesser figure, said the Captain.

My pig, my pig, yelled Mrs. Yellington.

Indeed, a most wholesome person without the slightest morbid insinuation of bacon or pork chops about its person. However, I lift my skirt, and what do you behold? A pair of exquisite boots polished to high luster. Do these boots speak of one who is not supreme in figure? said the Captain.

Mr. Peepingtomcock has an eye for the sensually endowed comparison, and though he is at great fault in his own figure, he might make the judgment as to the figures among us, more naturally endowed in beauty, said Mrs. Shoutington.

I think Mr. Wedlock has a lovely figure, whimpered the Caretaker.

If you do not keep your hands off my lower torso I'll beat you with my wedding slipper, screamed Mr. Peacock.

No no, how dare you make such an offer with my nightstick starving for such an opportunity? cried the Captain.

Captain, go away, cried Mr. Peacock.

But my figure? cried the Captain.

The servants will retire to those rooms set aside for them. And you, Captain, are dismissed, cried Mr. Peacock.

But my figure surely has come to some notice . . . This wedding gown . . . My boots . . . Do not forget my boots; surely they reiterate in praise of my figure? cried the Captain.

A Captain of Police wearing a wedding gown can only appear the sensually convinced fool, who, on lure of sexual promise, falls victim to syphilis, said Mr. Peacock.

He who wears a wedding dress shouldn't throw stones at someone else's dress, cried the Captain.

The poverty of your metaphor speaks to the vicious habit of the ignorant. My use of the wedding gown is quite within legitimate motive. That I was to be wed, first support in its favor. That the stand-in, in lieu of the unwilling bride was, by unusual chance, a man. Hence, the problem solved in the equitable compromise of the parties to be joined. That both being men, the wearing of each a wedding dress gave construction to a symmetry that took neither from the one nor the other, but complemented what was best in each, and gave moment to the sacrament of marriage, said Mr. Peacock.

But why do you say I have no figure? cried the Captain.

You have a physiological shape bounded by a skin. You are a lump of glandular vanity. But as for figure, in the sense of aesthetically sensual concern, you are without figure. You are no more noticeable than an ox browsing in a distant field. We see a vague bovine mass; we remark without true notice, an ox, said Mr. Peacock.

But the pig, the pig, yelled Mrs. Yellington.

Emissary from pigdom, so to speak; and gives rise to a disquieting awareness of its unique presence. And lo, the fires of the sensual hearth tongue up in sharpened appetite, cried Mr. Peacock.

Go to your room before you commit some terrible crime, cried the Maid.

Please, madam, allow him to commit a crime. I beg you not to interfere with my pleasure. His crime is my nightstick's candy counter. His crime is confection, cried the Captain.

How dare you seek to discipline my son? Is that not my pleasure? Have we not sufficient tools and motive? How dare you come into my house and seek to act with parental authority? screamed the Maid.

I only meant to protect the pig from imperfect love. But, putting that aside, would you make a quick appraisal of my figure? said the Captain.

You are divine of figure, no one takes that away from you. But if any punitive violence is to be committed on Mr. Badcock, I think the members of this household have first claim. He has run up quite a debt of spankings, owed to those who have suffered under his tyrannical raids upon our sympathies, said the Maid.

You quite misunderstand me. I did not mean that I would involve any of the swinish instrumentalities in the pursuit of the perfect. But, as it were, from afar to admire. Turning from its droppings, only that I might save devotion from disgust . . . , said Mr. Peacock.

Go to your room, cried the Maid.

Yes, go to your room, cried Mrs. Yellington.

Go to your room, dear, and take off your pretty dress, said the Caretaker.

You heard your parents, go to your room, said the Captain.

Mr. Naughtycock, you have indeed offended in your sensual remarks the desire on our part for a quiet and orderly existence. And I think it best you acted on the advice given, and retired. For further utterances may indeed bring down upon you a wrath not altogether deserved. But, however, well stoked by your ever insistence to turning all consideration toward the patently sensual. And it is most unfortunate that you should choose a time like this, when we find ourselves dressed in the purity of the white wedding gown, to bring forth matters sanctioned only to that privacy bounded by love, said Mrs. Shoutington.

But you see, however correct your verdict might be, it has been brought by persons illegitimately stationed on my property who have no right to judge what I do or say within these walls, said Mr. Peacock.


## MORALITY

However, morality goes far beyond mere property rights. And that you commit immorality, with or without deed to property, does in no way waive your responsibility to pay the debt on good taste incurred, said Mrs. Shoutington.

But I have been at war. You see, in times of war moral structures are apt to suffer ravages of the fury. In that arms have been taken up against me by wicked servants, so have I declared that a state of war exists between Mr. Peacock and the wicked servants, who in the first act of the conflict made off with a chair. Now a series of events follow, historic postures struck, each with aggressive intent. Servant menacing master. Master confounded, though undaunted by servants in numbers that bespeak defeat to the master. Still, does the master give way to hysterical research into his psyche? Does he explore the I-Ching for the moment of his measure? Does he go spooky and seek a spiritual victory. No, he seeks the victory of the athlete, by honorable sport. Victory without honor is the victory of the seducer, the chair thief, said Mr. Peacock.

But you are a proven seducer. You have only to look at my sister holding in her arms the product of the seduction, said Mrs. Shoutington.

She holds a pig, screamed Mr. Peacock.

Which is by symbol that which comes of the seduction, said Mrs. Shoutington.

No one says that the pig has not right in its presentation of moral claim. Presenting itself as a pig in no way lessens its moral instruction. But as to claiming direct lineage to the Peacock tree, that poses certain biological problems; which I do not put as definite impediment, but do regard as some source of disquiet. Whilst yet, quite concerned with the moral implication of its claim. Perhaps it is a Peacock. In such case I waive biology to moral purity, said Mr. Peacock.

To question whether or not it is a Peafowl is to dodge the question of parental debt owed the bastard. No, you cannot by words reduce the erotic abandonment of modesty, shouted Mrs. Shoutington.

I do not condemn the pig to being a pig. It might well advance up the ladder of humanness to a porkish humanity. No, I do not set aside the possibility of a great military career for the pig — Captain Pig, General Swine. Who knows but that the very course of human history may now be swerving into the barnyard through the dung heaps of the pigpen, along the foul chicken perch, hovering above the noxious cow platters? Who knows? Certainly I do not wish to stem the tide of the historically correct convergence of man and beast, cried Mr. Peacock.

Then you are willing to sign the deed of this estate over to the pig? The pig I am sure can be convinced to allow you a lifelong residence in the pigpen for your sensitive adherence to moral justice, said Mrs. Shoutington.

No no, that is quite contrary to the master's dignity. All lose respect for him wallowing in pig droppings. And it denotes by appearance the lowering of moral standards, if not decline altogether. Not to say that the relaxation afforded in the pigpen is not worthy of applause. Surely the porkish surrender to leisure bespeaks something of the noble. But to conduct the affairs of the estate from a pigpen . . . , said Mr. Peacock.

Shut up, said the Maid.

My nightstick is held at the ready, cried the Captain.

. . . But to conduct the affairs of the estate from a pig pen . . . The master is of simple tastes; a rustic nature given to wild bucolic moments, when not else than the simple station of the pig will do; or he betakes himself, as the chicken, upon a perch where the moonlight floweth like simple wisdom through the chicken house window. And there in that milky ray the cosmic musca domestica comes to him singing, said Mr. Peacock.

At the ready is my nightstick by virtue of the authority vested in its appetite, cried the Captain.


**AND SO TO BED . . .**


Caretaker, take Mr. Peacock to his room, said the Maid.

Upsy-daysy, Mr. Loviecock, said the Caretaker.

Put me down, screamed Mr. Peacock.

If my nightstick might be of service please do not hesitate to call upon it, cried the Captain.

He's carrying the bride to the nuptial couch, yelled Mrs. Yellington.

Put me down, screamed Mr. Peacock.

Upsy-daysy, said the Caretaker.

No no, the donkey must by subtle insinuation imply its need to bear the human burden, to give warmth to its back under the human sitting, cried Mr. Peacock.

Upsy-daysy, said the Caretaker.

No no, the donkey moves beyond its animalship if it lay hands on an unwilling burden, giving vent to its need to service, cried Mr. Peacock.

Take him to his room, cried the Maid.

No no, I am not to be taken to my room as if I were handled with the ease of that which is so handled. No no, I protest in the name of autolocomotion, self-determination, and in the name of democratic institutions, screamed Mr. Peacock.

Why do you stand there grinning, you horrible Caretaker? cried the Maid.

It is embarrassing to find the bride too heavy to lift up the stairs. It admits of her heft. It cries of her fatted indulgence. And it speaks no less embarrassingly to the weakness of the groom, that he cannot get the bride to the nuptial privacy, said Mrs. Shoutington.

What are you saying? screamed Mr. Peacock.

That you ought to be ashamed to let the Caretaker carry you away like a conquered bride. Why, he's old enough to be your father. Yet, you snuggle in his arms with all taste abandoned, screamed Mrs. Shoutington.

I have no wish for this adventure. You are quite ill-advised. And I take it badly that you would see in this unfortunate circumstance motivation on my part more than annoyance at being lifted as if I were something that is just simply lifted, cried Mr. Peacock.

Sir, you is got too heavy, whimpered the Caretaker.

Such a figure, so overridden with fat, said Mrs. Shoutington.

But in remedial discipline in the name of gruel and other muzzles to the beast of pleasure, cried Mr. Peacock.

Now do you see our problem of getting Mr. Peacock to bed every night? said that Maid.

Put me down, screamed Mr. Peacock.

You is got too heavy, whimpered the Caretaker.

I say put me down, or we shall both fall and our skirts blow up, screamed Mr. Peacock.

There ya be, said the Caretaker.

Don't you ever lay hands on me again. How dare you interrupt the master's relationship to the earth? It is not merely the physicality of the master, which is of central importance, but that he is separated from the earth in the arms of the servant. And by symbol, if not in fact, so the estate is seen to be held in the servant's embrace, cried Mr. Peacock.

I'm feeling rather fatiguè, said the Captain.

Well, go along with Mr. Peacock, Captain, said the Maid.

The master does not invite the Captain of Police to spend the night in his room, screamed Mr. Peacock.

I promise you that Mr. Praecox shall behave, said the Captain.

May I help? whimpered the Caretaker.

I think I am sufficiently schooled in police technique not to require the services of the Caretaker, said the Captain.

Then go along, both of you, cried the Maid.

I do not want this person in my room, cried Mr. Peacock.

Now that we are to be roommates I do wish you would break down and admit the significance of my figure. It would do you no harm to own up to it. Rather, it would serve to credit you. Though you are more heft than shape yourself, still, that you possess an eye to excellence excuses in large measure your own fault in the hierarchy of figures, said the Captain.

I suppose we will spend the night discussing your figure? screamed Mr. Peacock.

Oh, how wonderful that will be. The whole night! It shall be like a musical piece in orchestrated praise. An adventure in theater conducted with my nightstick, cried the Captain.

Mr. Squawcock, before you ascend you would do well to take one fast estimate of my figure, shouted Mrs. Shoutington.

I do not want to talk about figures. I am tired, tired, tired . . . So much so, that all sensual consideration is quite too other than my need to sleep; that even my moral judgment yawns without response to these incredible displays of erotic vanity. And again I must say that the physical presence of those of inferior station mark no more upon my awareness than the ox browsing in a distant field, yawned Mr. Peacock.

# Peacock's Wedding Trip

The Maid stood in the doorway of Mr. Peacock's bedroom and said, Mr. Peacock, dear, the arrangements are ready.

Arrangements? cried Mr. Peacock.

The wedding trip, roared the Maid.

In all the confusion did I get married? cried Mr. Peacock.

Only time will tell, said the Maid.

Doesn't the wedding trip seem a little premature? cried Mr. Peacock.

We've gone to a lot of trouble, roared the Maid.

But I was just going to sleep, yelled Mr. Peacock.

Not on your wedding night. Why, your dowry is ready, and the vehicle is at the front door. After all, it was very nice of the Caretaker to offer to drive you, said the Maid.

But, where? . . . The lonely bride is driven through the moonlight, widowed before her marriage. Besides which, it is discovered that the bride is a male athlete. The driven bride weeping from a carriage window is actually a heavily muscled man of honor; the bridal veil caught in the whiskers of his unshaven chin. It is all a terrible mistake, cried Mr. Peacock.


Suddenly the Caretaker stood in the doorway and whimpered, oh, no, sir, we would never think of hitting you with a hammer, even if the bride refuses to shave . . .

A hammer? What cruel image is that? screamed Mr. Peacock.

No no, to hit the bride on the head with a hammer, even though it consolidates the many spankings put off in service to the hope of remissible behavior; calling upon spanking as the last recourse . . . Hardly, of course, to be recommended by a person in my station . . . Not even to be entertained as a possibility . . . , said the Caretaker.

How dare you be so long-winded on such a momentous night? screamed Mr. Peacock.

I should think the hammer far worse than the nightstick, said the Caretaker.

These idle comparisons between items of violence . . . , screamed Mr. Peacock.

One is not always in a position to decide which tool would best serve at the time when the use of one is necessitated by events quite beyond the stage of threat or promise. When the bride has reached the point where the sheer weight of spankings owed the bride demands a quick solution in the form of a single blow, said the Caretaker.

But the bride is an athlete of huge musculature. And the Caretaker best beware, cried the Mr. Peacock.

. . . Only to say that one must be aware that even in the violent moment, there is still the choice to be made. One cannot simply pick up a hammer and think the proper tool has come to hand. One must weigh the possible use of a nightstick, or even a whip. Sometimes a whip is most useful in arranging the bride's temperament, said the Caretaker.

One sees how the master leads by clever contrivance the serving man to itemize his humble resources against the injustice of the harsh master, said the Maid.

The use of a hammer against a member of the ruling class? screamed Mr. Peacock.

The humble tool of the carpenter; he raises the pitiful tool of manual labor as a cry against the idle rich, said the Maid.

And brings it down with the force of many spankings compounded into a single blow. This is the humble carpenter. And what is he building beyond the punitive wound? screamed Mr. Peacock.

He hammers home the house of discipline. Each blow a nail of moral instruction, said the Maid.

What a terrible wedding night, said Mr. Peacock.

No no, you cannot overlook the sensitive concern of the Caretaker as to the proper tool of discipline; as is seen in the delicacy so expressed in his list of available instruments, said the Maid.

Oh, what is all this? I'm trying to sleep, screamed Mr. Peacock.

No bride rests on her wedding night, said the Maid.

I am not oblivious to natural law . . . If the ritual had any value, then of course the flight of the queen bee is thus prescribed. I would not move to counter the current of natural law, said Mr. Peacock.

Then bow to the household that sends forth its daughter in the name of the romantic imperative, that the inheritance might fall with more justice, cried the Maid.

The widowed bride rides through the moonlight, sighed Mr. Peacock.

The bride and her dowry set out in a wheelbarrow across the hills, said the Maid.

. . . And the barking of dogs, said Mr. Peacock.

. . . And flies drawn by the scent of manure follow thickly on the nuptial vehicle, said the Maid.

It is fitting that the flies follow on the nuptial flight of the athlete, debased and without consort; fallen from his proper gender, said Mr. Peacock.

Not that the manure doesn't play some part in attracting flies, said the Maid.

Manure? screamed Mr. Peacock.

Horseshit, said the Maid.

Horseshit? screamed Mr. Peacock.

Oh, please . . . On this august occasion . . . , sighed the Maid.

Quite right. The mind often takes a vulgar turning. As if the anchor of obscenity were thrown down from a flight of angels to moor against that final heaven-rested joy that must fill us with exquisite fear, cried Mr. Peacock.

Oh, shut up, cried the Maid.

The metamorphosis of athlete to bride, though only by symbol . . . Still, what is the human? Only a head full of jelly and symbol . . . The metamorphosis shakes the flesh from hard muscle into soft, inquiring woman's fear, said Mr. Peacock.

Shut up. My God, shut your mouth, cried the Maid.

Surely the appetite for honor waned. No wider application of the gentleman's persuasive presence . . . Then servants, as if oxen, fell from the bows of their yoke and turned back on the plowman . . . All, as it were, in a jelly of symbols. Now the plowman, tangled in the reins, and in flight from the wicked oxen pulls the plow in fear whilst the wicked oxen guide the plow and whip him on. Until he rise again through the head's jelly from the fecundating device to the accomplished harvest in a dream, cried Mr. Peacock.

If the bride fears the first embrace we applaud her modesty, said the Maid.

Only because in the first loss is the punitive remission over the athlete in the pursuit of honor on the playing fields of muscular skill . . . , cried Mr. Peacock.

The bed-wetter, who must earn spankings as his daily bread, screamed the Maid.

But if the chair had not been lost, then the king sat his throne, and all was well, cried Mr. Peacock.

Sometimes the chair is locked away since the child refuses the disciplined privilege, said the Maid.

It will wound the mind, screamed Mr. Peacock.

Something is lost if the child will not come to its inhibition. Then its pot is put away, only to reappear in later years as that which is lost, like the childhood of a man, said the Maid.

And acts the punitive remission over the athlete in his pursuit of honor on the playing fields of muscular skill; and so diminishes the animal-moment of love; putting impediment to the business career; losing him rein over Maid and Caretaker, screamed Mr. Peacock.

A bed-wetter who must earn spankings as his daily bread, and so a catalogue of punitive tools, said the Maid.

And so gruel and other paraphernalia become the remedial means toward the rebuilding of moral structures that sag as does the flesh, cried Mr. Peacock.

Not to mention the sensitive concern of the Caretaker as to the proper tool of discipline, listing with delicate care the available tools, said the Maid.

And now the bride, widowed, and yet within the romantic imperative as the final nervous adjustment, screamed Mr. Peacock.

And her dowry, gruel put up in an enema bag to be sucked out for her wedding breakfast; the disciplinary hammer wrapped in dwarf's underwear, to be turned over to the master of your next situation; your chastity belt; a bottle of mayonnaise, for you shall surely develop rheumatism. As is the mother so is the daughter; you shall be given to undressing in kitchens and covering yourself with mayonnaise whilst spied upon by old men . . . Such is the lot of the aging service woman, cried the Maid.

I can think of nothing more revolting than the serving woman with all her obese spheres overlapped and sagging, exposed thus in her nakedness; stark for lack of any beauty, screamed Mr. Peacock.

Enough; I have been spied upon enough by men in my medicine need to have appraised their wishes, cried the Maid.

Am I not superior to the ox who gained human appearance by grazing on some freakish herb? Obviously your superior; and am, therefore, no doubt correct in my estimate of you. I have never heard of a fat old woman walking about in the nude, covered with mayonnaise. I have let this pass without judgment because of my breeding. But now that you bring it up again, I am more than angry at the picture you present; inviting impure thoughts. What do you take me for, a conspirator in these tasteless adventures you feel called upon to repeat? Surely these sordid details have little bearing on the disappearance of the chair. I cannot help wondering if your main purpose is not to stir up wild sexual fantasies in me. Leading, God help me, to a proposal of marriage! screamed Mr. Peacock.

You've already said that. I remember your having said exactly that before, said the Maid.

Because my sentiments have not changed regarding these tasteless exposures that act the parody to beauty, screamed Mr. Peacock.

But you used exactly those words, said the Maid.

Well, what of it? screamed Mr. Peacock.

Can't you see the full circle? said the Maid.

## THE CHAIR

It is the chair, screamed Mr. Peacock.

Which is sometimes locked away because the child refuses the disciplined privilege, cried the Maid.

It will wound the mind, screamed Mr. Peacock.

Only to reappear . . . The Caretaker will tie it on your back, said the Maid.

What? Wings? Wings of the false angel? screamed Mr. Peacock.

The disciplined privilege. That which is the place of the maternal rage. Your potty-chair, cried the Maid.

The disciplined privilege shall be tied to my back? screamed Mr. Peacock.

Yes yes, the disciplined privilege tied to your back; the chair that was locked away reappears as the dowry, cried the Maid.

No no, it is too small, screamed Mr. Peacock.

Too small for what? screamed the Maid.

It is a child's potty-chair, screamed Mr. Peacock.

And is the disciplined privilege, which is tied to the bride's back as treasure, cried the Maid.

No no, the bride is not only the bride, which carries forth treasure on her back like a serving woman, but the athlete toned with extreme musculature. That he gives space on his back to a potty-chair is an act of pity, extended to one less fortunate, cried Mr. Peacock.

Less fortunate? cried the Maid.

It is a degenerate chair, cried Mr. Peacock.

It is the child betrothed, said the Maid.

It is a shrunken chair, no doubt from age. Surely the young handsome man may lend his broad shoulders in a vehicular way to the aging cripple? cried Mr. Peacock.

It is the groom that the bride takes upon her back. It is the groom which is seen properly astride the bride, said the Maid.

No no, it is an old crippled chair, no longer able to function as a lap for humanity's ass. So that I take it upon my back as one would take one's father for a romp about the countryside, screamed Mr. Peacock.

No no, it is the childhood betrothal, now to be consummated, cried the Maid.

How dare you presume that I would have that commerce that is between the man and the woman with this chair, which is old enough to be my father? screamed Mr. Peacock.

You fail to see the youth of the chair. It is small only because it is young. In the early sweet days you and this potty-chair were betrothed in the house of the maternal despair, said the Maid.

What do you take me for, a degenerate, that I would marry a chair? I seek the chair only to inhibit theft. But, that I would lie with a chair, as did the elder Peacock, and commit myself to that which is between the man and the woman. Hardly, my dear serving person. One has only to look at the chair to see, that even were I swayed romantically toward furniture, this chair hardly recommends itself, for it is obviously dwarfed. Not so much by its glands, but rather in its intent, which is petulant and childish. Besides which, it has suffered a wound, which only invites fecal procedures. There is a definite hole in its lap, from which a pot hangs in which the sacrificial stains to good taste remain. I find it an extremely harsh opinion on your part in assuming that I have found ample mate in this inferior furniture, said Mr. Peacock.

But it's your shit in the pot, screamed the Maid.

How dare you assume that I have had a romantic adventure with this furniture? Had it been a grand piano, or a lady's vanity table . . . But a child's toilet! Do you think I molest children? screamed Mr. Peacock.

Enough. If the unwilling bride leaves no quarter, save the resource of the spanking So be it, a honeymoon of spankings, cried the Maid.

No no, it is not a throne. A throne can be loved. And though he be less than his throne, still he will have come to high estate in that environment of the golden mount, screamed Mr. Peacock.

Enough enough, the groom is to be tied to the bride's back, screamed the Maid.

At least give me the option of sitting on the potty-chair, that I might press my proper gender. No doubt the groom rides the bride; however, I beg to contest the Maid's conclusion, screamed Mr. Peacock.

Your rump's too big, cried the Maid.

No no, let us see if the childish wrong might not come to rightful fruition. I shall force myself down into the disciplined privilege, cried Mr. Peacock.

No no, you will break it, cried the Maid.

No no, it is the glass slipper. I will squeeze into it, cried Mr. Peacock.

No no, cried the Maid.

Look look, it fits. Now dignity is mine; the kingdom comes to unity. In the throne is authority. It is not the king that carries the throne, it is the throne which is vehicular to the power of the king. And about him are servants humiliating themselves to his glory. Now the master secretly farts into the cushions of his throne, for he is in the repose of the highest authority, and none move other than they serve him. For there is nothing that is worthy, save that it be in his service, cried Mr. Peacock.

I'm washing the pig's underwear, perhaps you would like to douche in the laundry water? said the Maid.

No no, my throne, screamed Mr. Peacock.

You're sure you wouldn't like to douche in the laundry water? said the Maid.

My beautiful chair, my pedestal of authority, screamed Mr. Peacock.

Would you like me to pour the used laundry water over your head? It would be like a shower, said the Maid.

Get back! You may bow in reverence, screamed Mr. Peacock.

Would you like me to pour the used laundry water over you like a shower? You could clean your ears. said the Maid.

The king is seated on his throne, screamed Mr. Peacock.

It's a potty-chair, there's still some childish shit in the pot, said the Maid.

Bow before me, screamed Mr. Peacock.

I think it an extremely tasteless act on your part to have a bowel movement in the kitchen. It does little to recommend you to domestic service; rather, it acts the deterrent to further service, said the Maid.

Why are you not bowing, as so instructed? screamed Mr. Peacock.

The Caretaker has very thoughtfully agreed to cart you part of the way in his wheelbarrow. So, if you will just gather your dowry together, the punitive hammer, your chastity belt, and other oddments . . . Since he has a load of manure to move anyway, you might just as well ride part of the way, said the Maid.

The king will ride in a wheelbarrow on a heap of manure? cried Mr. Peacock.

Suit yourself. If you'd rather cover up in the manure, that's up to you, said the Maid.

Would you like to be covered up in manure? said the Caretaker.

Are you quite out of your minds, to suggest the king travels covered in manure? screamed Mr. Peacock.

Suit yourself. Cover yourself in horseshit if like. Your care and maintenance are entirely out of our hands now, said the Maid.

Do not break my throne, screamed Mr. Peacock.

You're breaking it yourself with your fat wedding gown, said the Maid.

No no, it is breaking because you are envious of it, screamed Mr. Peacock.

You're breaking that poor little chair, said the Maid.

It's breaking, it's breaking, my throne is breaking, screamed Mr. Peacock.

Well, get off of it, cried the Maid.

It's broken. There's nothing left, screamed Mr. Peacock.

There is always your chastity belt, said the Caretaker.

And there's this used laundry water, said the Maid.

No, the chair is broken. Nothing remains, wept Mr. Peacock.

The Caretaker will tie the pieces on your back, said the Maid.

No no, there is nothing, wept Mr. Peacock.

Well, you can still wear the pot on your head. Won't that be nice? Just like a little soldier girl, said the Maid.

No no, the king has nothing left, wept Mr. Peacock.

Well, you can pretend the pot is a crown. Won't that be nice? said the Maid.

No no no, cried Mr. Peacock.

There's always the sedative of the hammer, said the Maid.

No no, even if the inventory is run through again there is always a chair missing, screamed Mr. Peacock.

Well, it is just a chair, Mr. Pettycock, said the Caretaker.

No, it is not just a chair, it is symbolic. It creates the rent out of which all things flow away. The inheritor is disinherited, said Mr. Peacock.

Let me hold your train, said the Caretaker.

. . . What about the used laundry water? said the Maid.

**ABOUT THE BOOK**

This book was designed by Allan Kornblum, and was set in Co-chin type. The high resolution output was supplied by Hi Rez Studio. This book has been printed on acid-free paper, and has been smyth sewn for reading comfort and for added durability. Printing and binding by Walsworth Publishing in Marceline, Missouri.